L. RON HUBBARD

FORBIDDEN GOLD

Published by
Galaxy Press, LLC
7051 Hollywood Boulevard, Suite 200
Hollywood, CA 90028

© 2014 L. Ron Hubbard Library. All Rights Reserved.

Any unauthorized copying, translation, duplication, importation or distribution,
in whole or in part, by any means, including electronic copying, storage or
transmission, is a violation of applicable laws.

Mission Earth is a trademark owned by L. Ron Hubbard Library and
is used with permission. *Battlefield Earth* is a trademark owned
by Author Services, Inc. and is used with permission.

Horsemen illustration from *Western Story Magazine* is © and ™ Condé
Nast Publications and is used with their permission. Fantasy, Far-Flung Adventure
and Science Fiction illustrations: *Unknown* and *Astounding Science Fiction* copyright ©
by Street & Smith Publications, Inc. Reprinted with permission of Penny
Publications, LLC. Cover art: © 1935 Metropolitan Magazines, Inc.
Reprinted with permission of Hachette Filipacchi Media.

Printed in the United States of America.

ISBN-10 1-59212-272-8
ISBN-13 978-1-59212-272-1

Library of Congress Control Number: 2007903622

CONTENTS

STORIES FROM PULP FICTION'S GOLDEN AGE

AND it *was* a golden age.

The 1930s and 1940s were a vibrant, seminal time for a gigantic audience of eager readers, probably the largest per capita audience of readers in American history. The magazine racks were chock-full of publications with ragged trims, garish cover art, cheap brown pulp paper, low cover prices—and the most excitement you could hold in your hands.

"Pulp" magazines, named for their rough-cut, pulpwood paper, were a vehicle for more amazing tales than Scheherazade could have told in a million and one nights. Set apart from higher-class "slick" magazines, printed on fancy glossy paper with quality artwork and superior production values, the pulps were for the "rest of us," adventure story after adventure story for people who liked to *read*. Pulp fiction authors were no-holds-barred entertainers—real storytellers. They were more interested in a thrilling plot twist, a horrific villain or a white-knuckle adventure than they were in lavish prose or convoluted metaphors.

The sheer volume of tales released during this wondrous golden age remains unmatched in any other period of literary history—hundreds of thousands of published stories in over nine hundred different magazines. Some titles lasted only an issue or two; many magazines succumbed to paper shortages during World War II, while others endured for decades yet. Pulp fiction remains as a treasure trove of stories you can read, stories you can love, stories you can remember. The stories were driven by plot and character, with grand heroes, terrible villains, beautiful damsels (often in distress), diabolical plots, amazing places, breathless romances. The readers wanted to be taken beyond the mundane, to live adventures far removed from their ordinary lives—and the pulps rarely failed to deliver.

In that regard, pulp fiction stands in the tradition of all memorable literature. For as history has shown, good stories are much more than fancy prose. William Shakespeare, Charles Dickens, Jules Verne, Alexandre Dumas—many of the greatest literary figures wrote their fiction for the readers, not simply literary colleagues and academic admirers. And writers for pulp magazines were no exception. These publications reached an audience that dwarfed the circulations of today's short story magazines. Issues of the pulps were scooped up and read by over thirty million avid readers each month.

Because pulp fiction writers were often paid no more than a cent a word, they had to become prolific or starve. They also had to write aggressively. As Richard Kyle, publisher and editor of *Argosy*, the first and most long-lived of the pulps, so pointedly explained: "The pulp magazine writers, the best of them, worked for markets that did not write for critics or attempt to satisfy timid advertisers. Not having to answer to anyone other than their readers, they wrote about human beings on the edges of the unknown, in those new lands the future would explore. They wrote for what we would become, not for what we had already been."

Some of the more lasting names that graced the pulps include H. P. Lovecraft, Edgar Rice Burroughs, Robert E. Howard, Max Brand, Louis L'Amour, Elmore Leonard, Dashiell Hammett, Raymond Chandler, Erle Stanley Gardner, John D. MacDonald, Ray Bradbury, Isaac Asimov, Robert Heinlein—and, of course, L. Ron Hubbard.

In a word, he was among the most prolific and popular writers of the era. He was also the most enduring—hence this series—and certainly among the most legendary. It all began only months after he first tried his hand at fiction, with L. Ron Hubbard tales appearing in *Thrilling Adventures, Argosy, Five-Novels Monthly, Detective Fiction Weekly, Top-Notch, Texas Ranger, War Birds, Western Stories,* even *Romantic Range.* He could write on any subject, in any genre, from jungle explorers to deep-sea divers, from G-men and gangsters, cowboys and flying aces to mountain climbers, hard-boiled detectives and spies. But he really began to shine when he turned his talent to science fiction and fantasy of which he authored nearly fifty novels or novelettes to forever change the shape of those genres.

Following in the tradition of such famed authors as Herman Melville, Mark Twain, Jack London and Ernest Hemingway, Ron Hubbard actually lived adventures that his own characters would have admired—as an ethnologist among primitive tribes, as prospector and engineer in hostile climes, as a captain of vessels on four oceans. He even wrote a series of articles for *Argosy,* called "Hell Job," in which he lived and told of the most dangerous professions a man could put his hand to.

Finally, and just for good measure, he was also an accomplished photographer, artist, filmmaker, musician and educator. But he was first and foremost a *writer,* and that's the L. Ron Hubbard we come to know through the pages of this volume.

This library of Stories from the Golden Age presents the best of L. Ron Hubbard's fiction from the heyday of storytelling, the Golden Age of the pulp magazines. In these eighty volumes, readers are treated to a full banquet of 153 stories, a kaleidoscope of tales representing every imaginable genre: science fiction, fantasy, western, mystery, thriller, horror, even romance—action of all kinds and in all places.

Because the pulps themselves were printed on such inexpensive paper with high acid content, issues were not meant to endure. As the years go by, the original issues of every pulp from *Argosy* through *Zeppelin Stories* continue crumbling into brittle, brown dust. This library preserves the L. Ron Hubbard tales from that era, presented with a distinctive look that brings back the nostalgic flavor of those times.

L. Ron Hubbard's Stories from the Golden Age has something for every taste, every reader. These tales will return you to a time when fiction was good clean entertainment and the most fun a kid could have on a rainy afternoon or the best thing an adult could enjoy after a long day at work.

Pick up a volume, and remember what reading is supposed to be all about. Remember curling up with a *great story.*

—Kevin J. Anderson

KEVIN J. ANDERSON *is the author of more than ninety critically acclaimed works of speculative fiction, including* The Saga of Seven Suns, *the continuation of the* Dune Chronicles *with Brian Herbert, and his* New York Times *bestselling novelization of L. Ron Hubbard's* Ai! Pedrito!

FORBIDDEN GOLD

CHAPTER ONE

"THAT'S all you have to do, Mr. Reid. Just match this gold nugget and old Nathan Reid's money is yours." Kimmelmeyer looked legally at Kurt Reid and rolled the nugget in question about in his soft, plump hand.

Kurt Reid cocked his head a little on one side and took a long drag at a cigarette. Then he crossed his long legs and exhaled the smoke in a blue cloud which enveloped the desk.

Kimmelmeyer coughed, but his eyes remained very fatherly and legal. Compared to Kurt, Kimmelmeyer was small. Kimmelmeyer's head was bald, shining as though newly burnished with furniture polish. Kimmelmeyer's ears were elfinly pointed. His chin was sunk far down in a wing collar, giving his face a half-moon appearance.

"That's all I have to do," said Kurt with a twisty grin. "What's the matter, Kimmelmeyer, don't you like me any better than Nathan Reid did?"

"Like you?" gaped Kimmelmeyer, missing the point.

"You act as if I were about to go on a Sunday School picnic instead of a gold hunt in Yucatán. What if I don't want to go, huh?"

The legal look vanished. Kimmelmeyer stared amazed at Kurt. He did not feel at all at ease with this young man.

3

Something in Kurt's attitude was vaguely insolent. The man's poise was too astounding. No, Kimmelmeyer did not understand Kurt Reid. They were too many character miles apart. Gangly, good-humored Kurt, on his part, understood Kimmelmeyer a little too well.

"But Mr. Reid!" said Kimmelmeyer. "Have you no sense of proportion at all? Here I have just offered you a chance at four million dollars and a town house and a country house and what do you do? You sit there and ask me foolish questions about whether I like you or not."

"I knew old Nathan Reid," said Kurt, dragging at his smoke. "And as certain as I'm his grandson, he didn't intend to do any good by me through you. Besides, when you're running through soup and you're out of gas and you see a landing field, it's ten to one the thing's a bog and you'll get killed anyway."

"Ai! Don't be so pessimistic. I thought all pilots were optimists."

"I'm alive," said Kurt. "Optimistic pilots are all dead."

"But what can be wrong? See here, I bring you here at my own expense—"

"At Nathan's," corrected Kurt.

"I bring you here to show you the contents of his will and you aren't even glad about it. He says right here, paragraph three, 'Whereas, if said Kurt Reid sees fit to match this gold nugget in Yucatán, I designate further that he be given my entire estate.' Now what you want, eh? You want I should just sign these papers over to you now?"

"That wouldn't be a bad idea," said Kurt. "But come along.

Let's stop arguing about this thing. Does he say where this gold is down there in Yucatán?"

"No."

"Any bet he only gives me a month to find the stuff."

"That's right."

"And he makes no provision for getting me to Yucatán."

"What you want, eh?" cried Kimmelmeyer. "Can't you invest a couple thousand in return for four million?"

"Sure, but I haven't got a penny. Look here." Kurt raised his brown oxford so that Kimmelmeyer could see the sole. A hole was there, backed by a white piece of paper. "That paper is the letter you sent me," said Kurt.

"But I thought you had a good job on a transport line, eh?"

"I had one until two weeks ago. I stunted a trimotor when I was feeling good and the company didn't like it at all. In fact, they fired me. I'm flat and you'll have to give me the dough to go down there."

The request was rather sudden. Kimmelmeyer took several seconds to answer. "I . . . I'm sorry, Mr. Reid, but you see things are sort of slack and I thought . . ."

"I thought you were so hot to get me down there," said Kurt.

"Oh, I am! I am! I mean . . . er . . . should I not want to see you get all this money instead of hospitals and things maybe?"

"I don't know what the game is, Kimmelmeyer," said Kurt, squinting through the smoke, his silver-gray eyes studious. "Old Nathan Reid was my grandfather, yes, but he never liked me. He wanted me to study and follow in his footsteps, but I ran off and learned to fly. Furthermore, I was often sassy and

I seem to remember telling him to go to hell once or twice. He never appreciated that, someway.

"He hated me first because I was my father's son. He hated Dad because Dad went into the Navy and Nathan Reid was once thrown off the president's chair in Nicaragua by the United States Navy. He's got me all mixed up.

"Nathan Reid knew he could never get anything on me while he was alive. Now he's trying to do it after he's dead. He never had any scruples as a filibuster. He made enemies more than friends. After his Central American misadventures he tried to run everything by the same yardstick.

"You're just his mouthpiece, that's all. You don't know these things. I do. Nathan Reid wants to see me dead and I know damned well that a trap is waiting for me in Yucatán if I go down there looking for this gold. That pretty nugget you've got there still retains some of its quartz. That's rose quartz. The ledge is jewelry rock. Oh, I know my gold mining. If it's there, I can find it. Give me time.

"But here's something that you've never heard about. There's a saying about Yucatán and gold. The fact is known all around the Caribbean. You can look for gold in Yucatán. Gold comes out of Yucatán, brought by the Indians there. *But no white man that ever found gold in Yucatán ever got out alive except filibuster Nathan Reid.*"

"My God," whispered Kimmelmeyer.

"Nathan Reid hated me and now that he's dead he's trying to kill me. He knew that I'd go, and I'm going. I'm broke, but I'll make it someway. I know where he traveled in Yucatán.

Somehow I'll get a plane and fly over his old routes there until I find the place. I'm going to beat him at his own game."

The finality and earnestness of Kurt's last remark jarred Kimmelmeyer. In many ways, Kurt was like Nathan Reid. There was a certain positiveness about him, a certain gleam to his silver-gray eyes, a certain set to his lean, almost swarthy face.

Kimmelmeyer nodded. He had dropped the gold nugget on the polished surface of his desk. He had dropped it as though it had been hot. Kurt picked it up, studied it and handed it back.

Kurt stood up. "I'm going now. In a month—on the eighth of October—I'll be back here with a mate for that gold."

"Wait, wait," said Kimmelmeyer, once more efficient and legal. For a moment he had been transported to the seared plains of Yucatán, but now he was right back in New York with a solid chair under him, a newspaper and a big dinner waiting for him in an hour or two.

Kimmelmeyer picked up a copy of the *Eastern Pilot*, opened it and handed it to Kurt. "I was looking for your address and I got a copy of this," said Kimmelmeyer. "Look here, I just thought . . ."

Kurt read the advertisement in its neat little box. It said:

WANTED: A transport pilot, a radio operator and a mechanic for long flight. Two planes will be used, the duration of the trip will be six weeks or thereabouts. Destination: Yucatán.

Kimmelmeyer was eager, "There's your chance."

Kurt studied the man, grinned a little and then nodded. "Yes, here's my chance." He stuffed the magazine into the pocket of his tweed jacket and went out, slamming the door behind him.

Kimmelmeyer mopped his forehead and muttered, "Ai, but that was easy. Easy!"

CHAPTER TWO

KURT went to the address mentioned in the advertisement. The place was on First Avenue, close under the El. Shabbily dressed, sad-faced people loitered on the doorsteps, their voices drowned in the surflike roar of the El. Children scrambled in the gutters, pinch-faced and ragged. A huckster bawled a string of indefinite syllables in an assured tone and clanged his brass bell.

Kurt felt ill at ease, anxious to be away. People turned and looked at him as he passed. He did not belong here. He felt a sullen ill will toward him.

The door which bore the right number was painted green, sandwiched between a fruit stand and a scrap iron shop. A sign creaked overhead in the hot wind stating that apartments were to be had there by the day, the week or the month.

Kurt pushed the buzzer and the door rasped and clicked until he opened it. Then after he had passed, it still rattled. The man upstairs must be impatient.

Three flights up, Kurt found an open door. A man was standing in it looking at him. The man wore a vest which bore the signs of many hasty meals. He was unshaven, greasy of face and hands. The trousers he wore were peg-topped, flashily cut. The face also had the air of past flashiness, now worn through. The eyes were bulging, of indefinite color; the mouth was warped and cynical.

"Who the hell do you want?" he demanded.

Kurt stopped before the door and very carefully looked the man up and back down to the scarred shoes. He let several uneasy seconds elapse before he answered and then he said, "Who the hell wants to know?"

"Name o' Sloan," muttered the other, his poise gone.

Kurt took out the magazine and thrust it into Sloan's hands, pointing to the ad. "Have I got the wrong address? I'm thinking that I have at that."

"Oh, no, no. This is right. You a mechanic or a pilot or what?"

"I'm a pilot. I'm Kurt Reid. Shall we go in and sit down or shall we tell all to the neighbors?"

"Come in, come in," said Sloan, suddenly cordial. He led the way into a room blued with cigarette smoke. Two other men immediately bounced to their feet. A third person, smaller than the others, remained seated, watching with amused eyes.

Sloan did the introducing in an offhand way. "The fat guy is Bruce. This here guy is Bill Connelly. And that guy there I don't know. This here guy is Kurt Reid. He says he's a pilot."

Bruce took a quick step forward. His eyes were rather hazy behind silver-rimmed glasses. His shirt was well cut and the cuffs were stiffly starched and unbuttoned. His face was rather soft and sunburned. His hair was standing erect like combed steel wool. He was a foot shorter than Kurt.

Bruce offered his hand. "A pilot? Reid, you say? Very glad

to know you, very glad to know you. I suppose you've come to see about that position, eh?"

Kurt looked the three over. The fourth person definitely did not belong. A kid, decided Kurt, and a rather handsome kid at that.

"No," said Kurt, "I came down here because I like to walk. What's offered?"

"We're going to Yucatán," said Bruce.

Bill Connelly nervously blinked his eyes and said, "Yeah, Yucatán."

"That's right," agreed Sloan. "Yucatán."

Kurt grinned. "Oh, Yucatán."

Solemnly, the three nodded in unison. The kid in the corner smiled.

"Arch . . . archayologee," explained Bruce, wrestling with the word.

"Oh," said Kurt. "From some university, eh? You're professors, that it?"

Once more they all nodded. The kid in the corner laughed outright and they turned to stare. When their eyes came back to Kurt, Kurt knew that *they* knew he was laughing at them.

Bruce, after a moment's thought, evidently decided to let it ride. His hand came out of his right hip pocket. "Yes, we're going down in the interests of science. We have two planes, both of them very good, very fast, but we have only one pilot. That's Bill Connelly there."

Connelly's eyes were twitching. He swallowed a couple times, making his Adam's apple leap convulsively.

"The pay?" said Kurt.

Bruce looked at Sloan. Sloan's bulging eyes rocked toward Kurt and came back to Bruce.

"It's good," said Bruce. "A thousand dollars for the trip. And if you're the guy I think you are, then that ought to mean somethin' to you just now. You'll get it when you come back."

"While I'm down there," said Kurt, "I may want some time off to myself."

"That's okay," said Bruce. "You can even borrow one of our planes."

"And now how about me?" said the kid in the corner.

"He wants the job as radio operator," Bruce explained to Kurt. "Says he's pretty good. But I say he's too damned young."

Kurt looked fixedly at the kid in the corner. Young was the right word for it, unless . . . Kurt's silver-gray eyes were almost closed. A smile flickered on his mouth.

"Where's your papers?" demanded Bruce. "I gotta see your papers."

"I haven't got any, but if you'll take me to a key, I'll show you that I know my business."

"Where'd you get your experience?" said Bruce.

"I . . . uh . . . I was airline operator for TAT for . . . for three years."

Bruce snorted. "Nuts! You can't get a job by lying to me. You ain't old enough! Get out!"

The kid stood up and shot Kurt an appealing glance. "Maybe this gentleman could verify . . . see here, I've got a slip which shows . . ." The kid reached into a jacket pocket and brought forth a bundle of envelopes. Something silver flashed down to the floor, rolled halfway across the rug and stopped, spinning.

A compact.

Bruce stared at the thing, then at the kid. Kurt knew the answer instantly. This was no boy, but a girl. The face was more pretty than handsome. The voice was too fine for even a youngster.

Bruce loosed a muffled snarl. "You damned spy! Who sent you here? Who sent you?"

Bruce took two steps, feline steps. His hand gripped the girl's shoulder so hard that she winced. Bruce shook her, showing his teeth. "Who sent you here?" he roared.

The girl tried to answer, but the fingers hurt too much. She sagged forward, tears welled up in her eyes.

Kurt stepped easily to Bruce's side. He yanked Bruce around. No one saw the fist move, but the next instant, Bruce crashed into a chair clear across the room. Bill Connelly's jaw sagged.

Sloan yelped. His bulging eyes looked red. He stepped into Kurt with both hands clenched and swinging. Kurt weaved back and Sloan followed Bruce into the chair.

Bill Connelly was undecided. Kurt made up the man's mind. Bill Connelly crumpled up, a red welt appearing on his neck and jaw.

The three men were stacked against the shambles of the chair like a collapsed Indian tepee. They shifted, as though afraid to get up.

Kurt smiled at them. "I guess we'll get along, boys. I guess we'll get along."

Kurt turned to the girl, "Now, ma'am, let's let these fellows show us their planes and their radios. Time is speeding."

She rubbed her shoulder and then looked up at Kurt. Suddenly she laughed.

CHAPTER THREE

SEVERAL hours later, a sedan drew up before the Newark Airport Restaurant. Kurt Reid stepped out and Bruce handed him a five-dollar bill. The girl gave Bruce a questioning glance and then alighted at Kurt's side.

"I gotta arrange for the ships to be rolled out," said Bruce, now all complacent with the past incident apparently forgotten. "You stay here until we come around for you."

Sloan and Bill Connelly nodded politely and the sedan drove off across the highway toward the brown-and-white modernistic operations office.

The girl found herself ushered through the door and to a black-topped table on the right of the oblong mahogany-and-brass interior. She carried a small bag in her hand—a rather tattered bag from which she had produced a sport dress which she now wore.

Kurt looked at her hands. Capable hands they were, well trained, but right now they were shaking. The girl had a certain gray pallor in her cheeks, a certain listlessness in her dark blue eyes.

Without asking any questions, Kurt ordered a cup of black coffee for her. When she looked askance at him, he said, "You haven't eaten for the last couple days, have you?"

She lowered her eyes and nodded. Presently the coffee came and when she lifted it to her lips the ebon fluid ran down the sides of the thick white cup. Kurt took a sudden interest in the black-and-mahogany panels of the wall and ceiling.

Her eyes thanked him and she drank the coffee down. After that a little color came into her face and her eyes were less tired.

"Looks like we've hired ourselves a job," said Kurt. "What do you know about it?"

A platinum waitress hovered near, taking their orders. When she had gone, the girl said, "Very little. I saw the ad in the *Eastern Pilot* and I got down to First Avenue just before you did."

"Why are you taking a chance at it?" said Kurt.

She smiled; her mouth was tired. "Broke. Luck running against me."

"You really are a radio operator?"

"Yes, I really am. Six months ago I was the lead attraction for a flying circus. I turned a plane inside out every day for the crowds. A year ago I was copiloting a transport plane. Two years ago I was an airline hostess anxious to know all the ins and outs of a very mysterious, infinitely dangerous game. I know them now."

"You didn't tell me your name."

"It wouldn't mean anything to you. Nothing at all. I've heard of you, but . . . "

"That isn't telling me your name."

"All right, if you insist on the real thing: Joyce Sutherland. Joy Sutherland."

"I read about you someplace," said Kurt.

"You read that I crashed six months ago. They expected the old crate to hold together for ever and ever and when it went they told me I was a hoodoo. An airliner crashed with me in it. A parachute jumper was killed diving off my plane. And now with that on my name and with things as they are, there isn't very much chance of my coming back. It was a swift career, wasn't it?"

"And so you're perfectly willing to cast your lot in with Bruce and Sloan and Connelly."

"Funny thing about life," said Joy Sutherland. "If you don't work you don't eat."

Kurt did not smile. The tragedy of this girl was too deep. He knew what it was to be considered a hoodoo. No game is more superstitious than flying. Her name had gone before her. Hospital bills, left in a strange town, no friends.

"You come from the West, don't you?" said Kurt.

"Yes, San Francisco. How did you know?"

"The way you talk."

"You haven't told me anything about yourself, Mr. Reid." Her dark blue eyes were studying him. In a swift appraisal she knew him. He was a headlong chap with very little regard for the opinions of others. He was violent and gentle all in one. He was as tough as a drill sergeant and as soft as a girl. He was typical of a hard-eyed breed who had come into being with flight. Steady contact with danger, closeness of

17

eternity, had given him a careless attitude toward life. He knew things for what they were worth. Joy Sutherland knew and understood.

"I want to see Yucatán," said Kurt. "I never happened to have the chance to go there, and now that I'm on my uppers and my controls are kind of loose, I intend to give the country a squint."

"That's funny," said Joy Sutherland, staring at the two unwinking yellow eyes of her fried eggs. "Old Nathan Reid used to stamp around down there. I read it in the story of his death. You aren't by any chance . . . ?"

"His grandson," said Kurt, a little bitterly.

She took her cue from his tone. "I've heard about him before. Once the president of Nicaragua, unseated by the Navy, soldier of fortune, gold hunter, conquistador. From what they say he was a rather cruel individual."

"That doesn't describe him. He tried to break my father's heart and ended up by hating him because Dad went into the Navy. Now he's trying to . . ."

"But he's dead," reminded the girl. "Why speak of him in present tense?"

"Nathan Reid will never be wholly dead. He left his mark too deep in Central America."

She was plainly puzzled now. "But he was wealthy when he died. Why should his grandson have to take a rotten offer like this?"

"Grandfathers and flying circuses are a lot alike," said Kurt. "You and I are on the last lap of the flying trail. Perhaps I have a little more hope ahead than you, but unless I fly for sport I fly no more. Nathan Reid hated me. Down in Yucatán . . ."

She listened to his somewhat disjointed sentences, feeling something of the struggle inside him. When he left the explanation hanging in midair she did not press him further.

Bruce came, smoking a cigar, looking puffy and elated. "They're on the line. Come on out, Mr. Reid, and we'll see what kind of pilot you are. If the ships are all right and if you're all right, we'll start in the morning."

Kurt stood up and drew back the girl's chair for her. The three went across the highway to the hangars, walking silently, their gaze fixed on the two planes which idled on the runway.

One was a two-motored cabin job apparently capable of high speed. Her sides were gray and dull with long exposure. Her engines sounded well enough. She looked like a huge bug sprawled on the concrete, sunning itself.

The other plane was also a cabin job. It was yellow with a swayback and spatted wheels. Kurt knew the type well. Racy and compact, built for speed over long distances.

Bruce pointed to the smaller ship. "We'll take that one up, Mr. Reid, so you can show me how good you are. You'll probably pilot the bigger one and Connelly will have this one, I dunno. Anyway we'll see how good you are."

Kurt jackknifed himself and slid in under the control wheel of the plane. The ship had seen much service. Its panel was dented from a crash or two and some of the instruments were broken. However, Kurt had piloted worse in his time. He gave Bruce a grin.

"What am I supposed to do?" said Kurt.

"Just show me you can fly it, that's all."

"Transport license doesn't count for much with you, does it?" said Kurt.

"Take her off."

Kurt slammed the small ship down the runway. The bright disc of the spinning prop blurred the factory chimneys in the distance. The spatted wheels went light and came off. Kurt leveled out, gathering speed, and then sent the plane rocketing skyward in a steep climb. A glance sideways told him that Bruce was far from nervous.

Bruce kept his hands well away from the dual control wheel before him as though the thing might bite. He turned sideways and yelled in Kurt's ear, "Someday I'm gonna learn to fly one of these things. Then I won't need extra pilots for my expeditions."

The yellow ship banked and went around like a top, its under wing seeming to remain stationary in the sky below. Kurt whipped out of that and did a swift figure eight. He climbed and dived again. Through it all, Bruce's expression did not change in the least.

They were out over water now, with the waves looking crisscross and small below. Tugs and even steamers were mere chips in the water.

Without any warning, Kurt thrust the control column away from him. The monoplane nosed over, the engine began to scream as it revved up. Wires took on a whining note and the world loomed suddenly big through their down-pointed prop. A smile was flickering around Kurt's mouth.

The tugs grew larger. Men could be seen on their decks. Then the men had faces and finally hands and the yellow plane was yowling down at three hundred miles an hour less than five hundred feet above the waves.

It was a moment for swift action, but instead, Kurt took both hands off, both feet off and carelessly yawned.

Bruce screamed unheard into the din. For him death was a fraction of an inch away. His pudgy hands snapped out and gripped his dual control column. He eased back, his feet found the rudders and the plane fishtailed to kill speed. The nose came up, up, up until the wheels were rapping parallel to the waves, almost in them. Bruce, mouth compressed, eyes watery behind his glasses, began to build altitude. The yellow ship started up again with an easy glide.

When the altimeter was bobbing at a thousand feet, Bruce suddenly realized what he was doing. The plane wobbled and fell off on one wing. He overcontrolled. His eyes went beseechingly to Kurt's face.

With a very small smile, Kurt took his own controls and the ship slipped down to a smooth landing at Newark.

When he had cut the gas and the switch, Kurt turned easily in his seat and said, "Very nice work."

Bruce fidgeted with his belt, finally casting it off. "Anybody can do that if they're scared enough," he growled sullenly. He edged out of the cabin.

"And Mr. Sloan," said Kurt, "can he fly too?" Then he laughed loudly as Bruce scurried away.

Joy came to the step and looked up, questioningly. "What's up?"

"Bruce," said Kurt. "Something's wrong here. Very wrong. Bruce can fly. He's a natural. Connelly can fly. Maybe Sloan can fly. And yet they have to hire another pilot. Whatever these fools are up to, it's shady."

"You have to eat, don't you?" said Joy, amused.

"Sure, just as long as I don't have to eat too many bullets, I'm satisfied."

Sloan came over, his bulging, watery eyes very sad. "We leave in the morning, wise guy. Here's a ten-dollar bill. Be on time, get it? Six o'clock."

———

CHAPTER FOUR

THE airport was cloaked in gray darkness. The two-motored ship idled sluggishly, thinly seen across the runway. Gas was gurgling into the auxiliary tanks of the yellow plane. Sloan stood by watching, his face hidden in the collar of his extreme cut topcoat.

Bruce was hunched down in the cabin of the twin-motored plane, trying to keep warm. Bill Connelly was under the controls, his eyes batting, his fingers shaking. Bill Connelly nodded at the engines and climbed down, approaching the yellow ship.

A hand reached out of the grayness and detained him. Kurt Reid smiled and shook his head. "You're taking the big one out. I'm taking the little one."

Bill Connelly opened and shut his mouth like a landed fish. Then without a word he went back to the larger plane and conversed with Bruce in low, jerky tones.

Joy Sutherland, wrapped in a man's trench coat, came up to Kurt's side. "Good morning, Black Knight. I called your room when I woke up but you'd already gone."

"Had any breakfast?" said Kurt.

"I . . . I never eat any breakfast."

"But I gave you two bucks for chow," protested Kurt.

"I . . . I got me a permanent wave and a . . . a compact. I had to have them, Kurt."

"Never mind," he said with a grin, "I've got a hot thermos of coffee and some sandwiches in my grip."

"Which plane are you going to fly?"

"The little one. I couldn't stand to look at Sloan."

Bruce loomed out of the pea soup. "You're flying the big one, Mr. Reid. Them's orders."

Kurt turned around very slowly. "Your error, Bruce."

"My error, hell! Who's in charge around here anyway?"

"I'm flying the little ship."

Bruce sputtered and then saw the girl. "And we're not taking you. We decided we won't need any radio communication."

"The radio outfit is in the smaller plane," said Kurt. "She's going in that crate with me."

Sloan edged up, his hands deep in his pockets, his bulging eyes darting from Bruce to Kurt as though awaiting orders.

"No," said Bruce to Sloan, irritably.

Bill Connelly, batting his eyes, his mouth twitching, came over.

"She's going," said Kurt. "And I'm flying the smaller ship." His inky eyes went narrow with speculation. Then he added, "Or neither of us go at all."

"You mean you'll run out on us?" snapped Bruce.

"That's what I mean," said Kurt.

Sloan's hand in his pocket was moving up. "Put the gun away," ordered Kurt. "You can't do anything here on the runway and you're too yellow to do anything anyway. I see red when anybody pulls a gun on me. And if you shot me and I found out about it I'd really get sore."

"Aw, let him have his own way," growled Bruce. "Let him ride with the dame. But I'd like to know how the hell I can send messages with her in the other ship."

"Wig-wag 'em across with your ears," said Kurt.

The tension wore off a little. Bill Connelly edged toward the twin-motored plane and Sloan followed him. Bruce underwent a change and smiled.

"Okay, Mr. Reid, I was just joking anyway. Of course you can fly the small job. We stop in New York, Richmond, Atlanta and New Orleans. We spend the night there and then hop across the Gulf to Progreso, Yucatán—a distance of six hundred miles." He smiled uncertainly.

Kurt opened the door of the yellow ship and helped Joy in. Bruce departed for the transport plane. But as Kurt came around the nose he met another man he had not seen before. The fellow was dressed in mufti but there was something professional, even militant about him.

His words were few. "Watch them guys, buddy. You ain't one of them, I can tell that. But watch 'em close. They just missed getting a ten-year stretch at Leavenworth for kiting chinks across the border."

Then the fellow was gone, leaving Kurt to scowl through the gray mist after him.

Kurt climbed under the controls. The transport ship took off and Kurt followed, sending the yellow two-seater boring upstairs to greet the murky dawn.

Joy Sutherland had little to say. She had already discovered everything there was to know about the shortwave radio. She tuned in on the beam and connected the lights on the panel. Kurt felt a twinge of pride at her efficiency. He was more than glad to have her there, happy that he did not have to ride with the three.

He was not exactly sure of his position but he knew that he was somehow vital to the party. They weren't really afraid of him, not those fellows.

"She's riding kind of heavy," said Joy above the motor's full cry.

Kurt bobbed his head in agreement. Even an extra load of gas shouldn't make that difference. Joy did not weigh a hundred and ten pounds and his weight was less than a hundred and fifty.

Joy twisted around in her seat, unfastening her safety belt. A small space was behind the two seats and it was covered with a strip of dirty canvas. She pulled it aside, staring down in surprise. She tugged Kurt's sleeve, pointing.

Two light machine guns were there, their loaded belts coiled like a den of snakes all white and brassy. Kurt frowned. He saw something else. A sample pick, a shovel, a metal gold pan.

There was the extra hundred pounds. Looking up at the cowl, Kurt saw the slots and mountings for the first time. He felt a chill of uneasiness. Just what were they walking into? Machine guns, a gold pan . . .

That fact he had told Kimmelmeyer rose up again: You could dig gold in Yucatán but you couldn't take it away from there because of the Indians. Were the three going to try anyway? With planes and machine guns?

That was coincidence if he had ever seen it. Maybe too much coincidence. Something was wrong and amiss here someplace. He felt as though he were on the brink of a solution which he couldn't quite grasp.

Joy was wide-eyed. A flush of excitement was on her cheeks. Her mouth was slightly open, moist and pearly and scarlet. Kurt smiled her an assurance he did not feel.

First a dead man's trap and now a crazy gold expedition. In truth, all hell was waiting for him in Yucatán.

CHAPTER FIVE

RICHMOND, Atlanta and then New Orleans. All through the day Joy kept the beam coming in strong. Too far left for an N, too far right for an A, but most of the time Kurt slid down the invisible static highway with the signal coming in blurred and staccato, true on his course.

It was pleasant, skittering on top of the world at the level of the sparse white clouds. The fields were an immense checkerboard and the houses were dollhouses peopled by ants. The rivers were threads of silver on a minutely worked green tapestry. The mountains were frowning bumps, slashed and hacked and piled in long lines.

Over the Appalachians they struck a local thundershower which washed their wings and made them shine when the sun came out again.

But always drifting ghostlike beside them came the transport plane, a gray shadow, impersonal and detached.

And always with Kurt there remained the thought of Nathan Reid, filibuster, now dead. Nathan Reid who had carried the standard of a rabble army against the military autocracies known as republics in the ardent southland. And when he thought too long about it, Kurt's mouth would settle into a thin gash across his face—just as Nathan Reid's mouth had set those many years past when the going was rough and when an ambush was ahead.

Kurt retained no illusions about the romance of his grandfather. He had been young when he had first read Nathan Reid's journals. He had found them one day in the musty old attic lumped and forgotten in a corner of a field trunk. They had been bound with the Great Seal of Nicaragua—an over-ornate thing of comical rather than grand proportions.

He had read them, volumes held on his knickerbockered legs, with his grubby, small boy hands grimed with the dust of decades. The journals were too many for one reading and he had stolen back time after time to finally complete them. It had not been the romance which had made Kurt read those tomes. It had been sheer horror that had held him. Each time he read his stomach would twist uneasily within him and his dark eyes would grow large and afraid. He had marched in imagination with that rabble of Nathan Reid's and Nathan Reid had stinted nothing in setting down the chilly terror of the facts.

This man dead with gangrene, that one shot for theft, another murdered by his fellows. And the thick, oozing decay of the jungles running like a trail of slime through it all. Nathan Reid had dreamed empire and like so many men who have since become haloed saints in history, Nathan Reid had played his part—that of a brutal, single-purposed, egotistical bully.

This man he had shot with his own hand. This native he had tortured for information. This town he had burned through military necessity—and that pallid excuse for savage excess was painted well in the smeared, aging pages.

Young Kurt's back had smarted many times—too many times. Young Kurt had absorbed the bitterness of his father toward a military martinet, a despot who knew nothing save his own will, whose world was black save for that section which became illumined by the fire of his ego.

And now Nathan Reid was dead—as dead as that rabble he had led into the southland. But Nathan Reid could not abide death and here, weeks after the clattering fingers had taken him, he was still holding court over Kurt's destiny. The thought was gruesome. Nathan Reid was laid out nicely in a black frock coat in an exclusive cemetery, in an ornate mausoleum. But as far as Kurt was concerned the man still barked his imperious orders and glared with his inky, brittle eyes.

Had it not been for the presence of Joy, Kurt would have become very melancholy, following the ups and violent downs of his temperament. But Joy was seated serenely on his right, her eyes suddenly sparkling with interest at some sight below.

Her sport suit had seen better days, but it was far from shabby. Rather it had an air of respectable dignity. The color was blue, matching her eyes and the open-throated shirt was buff, matching her hair.

Joy was not beautiful in a fragile, insipid way. Her face was firm and round and frank and her mouth was made for laughter rather than pouts.

When evening came, Kurt was tiring. Without question, Joy took the dual control and flew with a graceful ease and unconscious smoothness which made Kurt wonder at her inability to get a job. But then, Kurt had always said that the greatest danger in aviation was starvation, and Joy had become branded as a hoodoo—as Jonah had been branded as a Jonah but had been nonetheless saintly for it.

The Mississippi curved over the horizon, a dozen twisting slashes of gold across a flat, brown world. Lake Pontchartrain shimmered under the slanted rays of the sun as big as an ocean decked with curving prows and fluttering sails.

The transport ship came down and circled the square field and then slid in for a cautious, almost stealthy landing.

Kurt sent the yellow ship down in a hissing sideslip which straightened out only when twenty feet separated them from the earth. The two-seater whistled just above the ground, floating, losing speed, to suddenly crunch down for a precise but somehow devil-may-care three-point.

Bruce was at the side of the yellow ship almost before it had stopped rolling. He opened the door and peered anxiously in. But the canvas appeared not to have been disturbed, nor did either Joy or Kurt mention the discovery of the machine guns.

Bruce smiled up as far as his flat, bulbous nose. There the smile stopped. "I'll attend to the hangaring of the ships, Mr. Reid. You and the dame . . . I mean Miss Sutherland can go uptown. Report back here about six tomorrow morning."

Kurt slid out of the cabin, stretching his long length and flexing his arms. "What'll I do for money? I'd like to have a hundred on account, Bruce. I've got to get some clothes."

Bruce scowled. "I can't . . ."

"Then," said Kurt, stifling a wide yawn, "I'll have to withdraw from your entourage, I'm afraid."

Grudgingly, Bruce drew out his wallet and counted a hundred in tens into Kurt's hand. Once more Kurt was surprised at this evidence that he was wanted very badly in the party. He wondered just how far this sort of thing would go.

"And Miss Sutherland would like an advance on her pay, too," said Kurt. "She ought to get about three hundred for this trip. You can let her have seventy-five now."

Sloan was slipping up toward Bruce's elbow. He shot a meaning glance at his boss and then licked his lips nervously.

Bruce tried to stare Kurt down. He saw the threat in Kurt's eyes. Not only the threat of leaving.

Bruce counted out seventy-five. Kurt laughed out loud at the slowness of the man's movements. Joy smiled and took the money.

Then without looking back, the two climbed into a taxi and headed off toward New Orleans.

"You've got him scared," said Joy.

"I wish I was certain that was it."

The cab deposited them on Canal Street and they stood for a few moments at the curb looking up and down the straight thoroughfare as though undecided where to go. Finally Kurt led the way to a store which was still open.

They separated at the entrance with a promise to meet there in half an hour. Kurt made his way to the men's clothing department and made known his wants.

The items he bought were of the greatest need: a pair of high, soft lace boots, a pair of light whipcord breeches, a broad-brimmed gray felt hat and a pair of light shirts.

Walking down the counter past the sporting goods section, he saw guns on display inside the shining case. He stopped, struck by a sudden idea.

"That Colt .45," he said to the clerk. "Can I have it now?"

"Well, it's a little irregular, but . . ."

"Give me a box of shells and five extra clips." Then with the gun bulging under his coat, he felt somehow safer. One never knew what would happen. Nathan Reid, Bruce . . .

Joy was waiting for him, giggling like a very small girl. "Tonight," she said, "you're going to take me to dinner, and then we're going someplace and dance. I just couldn't resist a dress I saw although I know I'll just throw it away after tonight."

Kurt looked at her, slightly amazed.

She stopped laughing, something like tears came up in her eyes. "It's . . . it's not often I'm happy, Kurt, and tomorrow you and I are going south across the Gulf to Yucatán—to God knows what. I . . . I have a hunch, Kurt, that . . . that we're never coming back."

The chilly statement sent a shiver down Kurt's straight spine. He forced a smile. "Forget it, Joy. Forget it. Tonight we'll find a place where there's music and good things to eat and maybe moonlight and we'll forget all about everything, huh? Just you and I."

She brightened, remembered her dress and began to chatter

with him about small but interesting things. Kurt walked silently beside her, listening to her voice, shouldering their way through the crowds. The Colt .45 banged against his ribs with every step.

CHAPTER SIX

PROGRESO, Yucatán, in the later Empire of the Mayans might conceivably have lived up to its name, but through the sleepy passage of centuries it had grown more and more dormant until at last it represented a typical Central American village living only for its afternoon siesta.

It is situated between two long lines of sea sand dunes, built on sand. To the north lies the restless blue of the Caribbean and to the south lies the low tableland—and all the forgotten mystery of the Mayans, all the sullen danger of untamed tropics.

The two ships landed on a smooth strip of beach and were immediately surrounded by crowds of natives dressed in abbreviated cotton shorts, white cotton jackets and Mexican straw headgear.

Bruce, alighting with nervous haste, brushed the crowds aside and went stamping down the beach, leaving dents in the sand with his heels. Bill Connelly batted his eyes and remained under the wheel of the transport. Sloan thoughtfully roved his eyes over the hybrid assembly about the planes.

Joy looked at the people and found kindness in their faces. Bananas, pineapples, strange green fruits with pulpy orange centers—the carelessly slung baskets presented a lure for her.

She climbed down and spoke to a yellow-skinned native in Spanish.

Kurt was surprised at the fluidness of her speech. He knew something of Spanish; he had always prided himself upon his knowledge of it. But Joy was talking like a native.

The natives understood quite a little of her speech. Their own language was a crisscross patois of Indian, Spanish and Mexican. But what they did not understand in her words, they took from the tone of her voice—a quality of language plundered by the printed page, a universal passport no matter what language is spoken. They also understood her eyes.

Many baskets were offered. These people had seen one or two planes before; they had seen a few white women; they had seen enough of life along this tropic strand to understand much they could not put into words. They sheered away from the transport plane and centered their attention on the sleek yellow ship. It was as though the gray bimotored job had smelled bad.

A man in a small flat-topped straw hat carrying a cane and stroking a flowing white mustache came up to Joy with a bow. His words were in the purest of Castiliano.

"You go far into the interior?" he asked.

"I don't know," replied Joy with a quick smile.

"Perhaps you go to Quintana Roo, eh? I ask because I have seen others go before."

"What is the matter with Quintana Roo? What *is* Quintana Roo?"

"The southern portion of the peninsula," replied the Spaniard. "It is an unknown fastness. I do not know just why it should attract the people of the north—except perhaps for the gold. I beg your pardon for asking in idle curiosity."

"No, no," said Joy quickly. "I am pleased that you interest yourself. What about Quintana Roo?"

"Oh," vaguely, "many have gone, few have ever come back. It is the last stronghold of the Ancients. The Indians there for long dwelled in this more equitable section, but when the Spanish crushed their revolts time after time, the Indians moved back away and out of sight, losing themselves forever in the jungle and on the plateau.

"You know of the early Spanish, yes? They tried to penetrate Quintana Roo and found it impossible. The Indians live there in peace—or perhaps their idea of peace. *Ave Maria, señorita,* but they went to long odds to obtain that peace. How they use it we do not know. But there is gold there. Sometimes it comes out. Sometimes we see huge nuggets brought by Indians.

"But we who live on this barren coast have grown cautious. We no longer try to push back into a territory which will not have us. We leave that for the people of the north. People such as that great *filibustero* Nathan Reid."

"You know of him?" said Kurt with quick interest.

"Know of him? By all the saints, *señor,* you must be joking. He is a legend here. Why, once he anchored in this very harbor. He saw a nugget from across the peninsula and he disappeared with a dozen of his men. Weeks later he came back, *alone*. But he had a nugget with him. A piece of gold studded with rose quartz as though he had ripped it from the vein. I was a little boy then, but I remember."

Kurt experienced a queer wave of unreality. He had seen

that same piece of quartz on the desk of a bald-headed shyster as carelessly handled as a paperweight. That bit of sun metal had cost the lives of a dozen men. And it might well cost the lives of thirteen.

He was about to say something about it when Bruce came back. Bruce was sweating and fuming, nerves raw with the indolence of the place. White men like Bruce had experienced the same fever for centuries. They had raved and fumed and had soothed themselves with alcohol and then had ceased to care even when the tropics finally got them.

"The dumb so-and-sos," rapped Bruce. "We can't get gas until morning! We'll have to stay here overnight."

"How long do we fly tomorrow?" said Kurt.

"It's a hundred miles to Quintana Roo," growled Bruce. "We could have made it tonight. I'm sick of this damned job. The sooner it's over the better." He stamped over to the transport plane and explained things to Sloan and Connelly.

The Spanish gentleman looked askance at the squat Bruce and then—perhaps it was because Joy smiled—he did that thing which Spaniards are always supposed to do and don't. He offered Kurt and Joy the hospitality of his house for the night.

They left the yellow plane under the guard of a ragtag, bobtailed soldiery who had come yawning from their barracks and who stood in the shade of the wings, rifles held awry, feet spread wide, splayed bare toes gripping the sand like a monkey's.

The Spaniard's hospitality was excellent, his house was beautiful, his wife was complacently plump, smoothly gracious.

Joy and Kurt were driven out to their ship in the small hours of the coming day, greatly refreshed, feeling for the first time a sparkle of adventure. Perhaps that came from the awe in which the Spaniard held them.

After all, they did look like a romantic pair. Joy's shopping in New Orleans had netted her laced boots and a riding skirt of white piqué, a broadcloth shirt, and a white hat which looked immensely impractical but which was not.

The tanks were being filled when they arrived and Kurt kept well away from the three self-styled scientists. He didn't wish to break the tranquility of the moment, the illusion that everything was well. Somehow contact with the three made him feel cheap.

He filled in a few minutes by removing the glass from the doors and side windows of the yellow ship's cabin. "It's too hot," he explained to the Spaniard. But to do this, he had to sacrifice the comfort of his gray felt hat. From his small bag he took a helmet and a pair of goggles.

Joy exclaimed her pleasure at the sight of the helmet. "It's funny! Where did you get that thing?"

Kurt smiled. "You ought to know. It came from your beloved California. Chinese, I guess. I received it from an aged fellow who used to take my plane every few trips."

He held the helmet out so that she could see it better. It was made of heavy material, soft as kangaroo hide. Embroidered and painted along the crest of it, so that the tails came down to twine about the ear pads, was a great fire-spitting dragon.

It was one of those things a pilot likes to acquire as an offering to the dangerousness of his trade.

41

"It's good luck," said Kurt, and was then instantly sorry.

Joy's gaze was averted. She pretended to take an interest in the natives who were straggling out of their huts in the early dawn. Kurt had reminded her that she was supposed to be a hoodoo. It was painful—this seriousness in superstition—as adolescent as the profession of flying itself.

They took off in a blasting cloud of sand. The transport ship was leading the way now, flying low and fast as though anxious to reach its destination without any more loss of valuable time.

They flew for an hour. On the ground it would have been a trek of a week's duration, perhaps more. But here in the clear blue air they devoured miles in the breath of seconds.

Henequen fields, acres of bayonet-pointed plants, fled away under their downreaching wheels. Roads gave way to ox trails and then there was nothing but blank ground, verdant expanse, tangled and meaningless.

They came to a high plain, flat as a table, an admirable landing field. The transport ship headed down and landed in a geyser of dust. The yellow ship followed and came to a stop a dozen feet from the stretching wings of the giant.

Kurt got down. It was hot with a shriveling heat. It was windless and depressing. The silence of empty miles closed in upon them, ringing in their ears.

Sloan came out of the big ship first. His bulging eyes were fishy but his trap mouth was set. Bruce followed him, walking stiff-legged like a stalking wolf. Connelly sat under the controls, waiting.

Kurt had not had time to realize what was up. He had no

warning whatever. A blue, ugly gun glinted in Sloan's grimy fist and the muzzle was unwaveringly centered on Kurt's chest.

"If he yipes," said Bruce, "give it to him."

"What the hell . . . ?" began Kurt.

Joy gasped, one foot still in the fuselage stirrup, blue eyes wide with fear for Kurt.

"Okay, Reid," said Bruce. "We're here. We're in the most deserted section of Quintana Roo. If you want to yell, yell. It won't do you no good. You asked for all this and you're going to get it." He waited for that to sink in. His glasses were flashing in the sun, his shirt clung to his back with sweat.

"You're Nathan Reid's grandson. You're down here to find a ledge of gold ore. I know all about you—*all* about you. Now spit it out and quick. *Where is that ledge?*"

"Tell Sloan to put that thing away," ordered Kurt, eyes as black as ebony, as hard as obsidian. His mouth was closed to a thin line and he spat his words through his teeth. "If you want information from me, you can go bark for it. Did it ever occur to you that I didn't know anything about this ledge?"

Bruce snorted in derision. "Turn around."

Instead, Kurt advanced a pace, straight at the gun. Sloan slanted a questioning glance at Bruce but the muzzle didn't waver.

Bruce also advanced. He shook his arm up and down and a leather-jacketed sap slid out like a stubby snake to hang by its wrist thong against his hand. Bruce juggled it. Kurt came on.

"Don't!" cried Joy. "Kurt! Come back! They'll kill you!"

Bruce sidestepped with a quick motion. The sap moaned through the air, missing Kurt by a fraction of an inch.

43

Sloan's face was completely dead as though he had never felt an emotion in his life. His bulging, codfish eyes were utterly impersonal. He aimed at the fleshy part of Kurt's thigh and fired.

The impact of the bullet turned Kurt half around. His leg crumpled. He went down, swearing, with a coil of powder smoke drifting about his gaily helmeted head.

CHAPTER SEVEN

JOY ran swiftly to Kurt, afraid that he was dead. She was not reasoning logically in that she gave no thought to what her own fate would be with Kurt out of the race.

The dry dust was swirling in a cloud about the fallen man and for a moment no one realized that Kurt was rolling over and over, plunging sideways from Sloan's gun.

Abruptly a stab of white lightning ripped out of the tan fog. Sloan's automatic leaped back away from bloodied fingers and landed with a small thump on the ground. The blast of Kurt's shot was deafening, but the voice which followed it was more like the thunder accompanying the lightning flash.

"Keep away from your guns!" roared Kurt. "Damn you, stand still!"

Sloan was backing swiftly. He stopped, shaking his hand to rid it of the pain, sending a fine spatter of blood over the sand. Bruce, goggle-eyed and gasping, stayed where he was. Connelly, unseen by Kurt, twisted about in his seat in the transport plane and fumbled nervously through the pile of dunnage.

Kurt came cautiously to his feet, still holding the .45. Joy was there beside him, holding him up. They backed slowly toward the yellow ship. Sloan, whimpering, watched them go without protest. Bruce's lips were moving in a slow monotonous fashion, cursing them.

Joy mounted the stirrup and helped Kurt into the ship after her. She flipped the booster and the engine started with a mounting whine.

Connelly found what he was seeking. It came up blue and shining.

"Hey, you!" cried Connelly. "Stop!"

The command went unheard in the blast of the yellow plane's engine. With Joy at the controls, the ship was already moving forward.

The light sub-Thompson in Connelly's hands began to chatter. Bits of dust flecked away from under the belly of the ship. Fabric vibrated under the onslaught of lead. The rudder slammed hard over, hammered there. The yellow ship careened into a right-angle turn.

The dust which arose from the skidding tail partially obscured the ship for a moment, but when Connelly saw it again it was flying free, headed up into the wind, wheels turning idly under the past momentum of the ground.

They were gone.

Bruce whirled about, his face red and furious. "Don't stand there like a fool. Spot the direction of their course."

"They got the machine guns," protested Sloan, nursing his hand.

"They . . . they what?" stormed Bruce.

"The two machine guns you said to put in that ship."

"I told you to take them out!" Bruce roared.

"I tried to, but I was afraid a customs man would see me or something. Honest-to-God, Bruce . . . oh, my hand!"

Kurt was engaged in an inspection of his leg. He could feel a trickle of blood going down his thigh. With a pocket knife he slit away the cloth over the wound. Then he smiled.

"Nicked, that's all," said Kurt.

Joy looked relieved. She was jockeying the plane through buffeting hammers of heat lift, gaining altitude as swiftly as possible.

"Where away?" said Joy.

"I don't know exactly." Kurt found a roll of bandage in the dunnage and in spite of the close confines he was making fair progress with the dressing. The iodine was making him wince as he covered up the graze.

That done he looked out across the endless land, gathering his wits. Back in his knickerbocker days he had read something in those old records of Nathan Reid's. Something about a lake of great size, two mountains like a gunsight, and a country slashed by deep ravines. Something about gold. He wished he could remember exactly where those mountains were. But the thought was hazy and incomplete. Nathan Reid's adventures in this locale had been harrowing enough.

He resorted to a map of the country. The surveyors had guessed at many things, using the things they had heard rather than seen. Quintana Roo seven or eight centuries after the Later Mayan Empire was still a lost world.

But he found the lake marked in blue and he found two

marks like asterisks which meant mountains. He was elated, though he was far from sure that these markings would lead him to anything like a gold vein.

He was glad of this break with Sloan and Connelly and Bruce. It had given him the excuse he wanted. It had been a shock to hear that they were after Nathan's gold, and he knew they would hardly let the matter drop where it was, but he was glad all the same. Of course, he'd hear from them later.

"Course due east," he told Joy, pointing at the black compass bowl.

"Aren't you going back to Progreso?" said Joy, yelling in his ear to make herself heard above the drumming engine.

"No, I'll explain later."

For a plane it was a small country. On foot it was huge. In a matter of minutes they had sighted a mountain. Joy sliced toward the peak.

Kurt sat eagerly forward, watching ahead. There should be another mountain there, close beside the first. And below them he should find a lake.

And there it was. Two mountains. He sighted the ground about them, watching for a glint of blue. This was too easy, too easy. The lake was spread out like a sheet of beaten metal, quiet and serene and completely forgotten—or so it appeared.

He took the controls then, forgetting his leg in the excitement of the discovery. His eyes were sparkling and alive and his mouth was drawn into a tight smile. Nathan Reid had not counted upon such ease. Of that Kurt was sure. Nathan Reid had wanted him to slog across the jungles in painful search.

The yellow ship cruised over the lake while Kurt inspected the terrain below. He frowned as he saw something which looked like a human habitation. He had heard much about these Indians. About their revolts and their wild return to the land and cities of the forefathers in Quintana Roo.

The thing he saw looked like a pyramid—was a pyramid with its sides ascending in steps to a square structure on the very top. Mayan architecture. Heavy stone statues of the feathered serpent. He noted that the stone appeared worn and that trailing vines were absent.

But then that might be some trick of growth rather than an indication of habitation.

Joy was staring down with parted lips, astonished at the structure, completely forgetting the present in the favor of that long-gone past. She remembered what she had heard of the Later Mayan Empire. Human sacrifice, terrible rites, the cruelty of the jaguar.

Kurt was interested in the place only as a landmark. There were other buildings down there, partially hidden by the brush, solid and blocky. This had once been a thriving city but now—or so it appeared—it was reclaimed by jungle.

The yellow ship spiraled lower and lower toward the top of the pyramid.

Suddenly Kurt yelled. Joy stiffened, brought back too swiftly from her imaginings.

Kurt was pointing down at the structure. The yellow plane went round and round, one wing motionless, spinning without losing altitude.

A streak of yellow had shined briefly there.

Kurt cut the engine. "There's gold! That means there's a ledge of it around here someplace. They wouldn't carry it far. That means we're right!"

Joy didn't have the slightest idea of what was behind all this but the thought of yellow metal thrilled her.

Kurt shot the power on again and the ship went hurtling back into the blue. Kurt looked around, watching for a black speck in their element which would proclaim the coming of the transport plane.

Then he dived in once more upon the pyramid. The lake had left a sandy stretch of beach beside it which might conceivably be used as a landing field in a pinch, but Kurt passed it by. Something was warning him not to land.

"If I could only get some of that," he muttered, looking at the yellow flecks of sunlight down in the temple. "It might be the same gold."

The plane went around in a tight bank, almost touching the top of the pyramid with its left wing. Kurt stared at the structure which was whizzing by so swiftly. He reached out his hand as though he could breach the gulf and take the temple away with him.

Then he looked at Joy. She was regarding him with a wide-eyed stare as though she thought him completely insane.

Kurt leveled off and drove upward again to the altitude of a thousand feet. Several miles away he could see a clear stretch of sand. He would land on that and look the country over. Certainly the vein was here somewhere. He would have to match that nugget in Kimmelmeyer's office—that nugget with its identifying streaks of rose quartz still imbedded in it.

The country was slashed by a hundred ravines, deep and dark as though hiding their contents from the morning sun.

The yellow ship went swiftly in for a landing. The ledge had looked wide from afar but here it was apparent that it was flanked by two ravines which left only thirty feet between them. A thirty-foot runway is sufficient if it is long enough, but as he neared the spot it became obvious that the landing would be a tricky affair. The hot and cold summits and depths were making a shambles of the air currents. The wind was rocketing away from cliffs and shooting straight up or ramming straight down again.

The ship was bounced like a rubber ball. Joy watched the runway below as Kurt came in.

The wheels seemed to fumble for the ground. Kurt fought the controls, right, left, right, forward and back, trying to maintain a balance.

It was crosswind and they kept drifting over the edge. Kurt went around and came back again, eyes very hard with the effort.

Suddenly he sent the plane down in a quick pass at the ground. The wheels struck, bounced and struck again. The edge was almost within reach of their fingertips. Kurt held them on the runway with his motor and his rudder.

At last they stopped rolling, one wing over the ravine. Kurt climbed out, flexing his stiff leg, looking about him. Joy remained in the ship, feeling weak after the effort at getting down.

"What's this all about?" demanded Joy.

Kurt realized then that he had told her nothing of all this

even though she was embroiled tightly within it. He came back to the stirrup and smiled at her.

In a few tense words he told her about Nathan Reid, about the gold nugget that had to be matched.

"But," she protested, "there was gold on that pyramid. I saw it. Why not get some of that?"

"I don't think it's from the vein," said Kurt. "I've got to find a gold nugget with the rock still clinging to it. Otherwise I miss out on four million, a town house, a country house, and God knows how much more. It's worth the try."

"I should say it is," she said, dazzled.

"Well, then, let's be up and doing. I've only got about twenty-eight days in which to find this thing. And by the shades of Nathan Reid, I'm certainly going to find it."

CHAPTER EIGHT

T HE country might have looked small while they were aloft, but now that they started down a ravine with the terrifying solid height of the canyon walls, they began to have some conception of this silent immensity. They spoke little going now, partly through the precariousness of their descent, partly through the solemnity of the tomblike silence which was relieved only by the dismal moan of the wind finding its way through the giant gray boulders and the clattering harsh green leaves of strange trees.

Kurt, in his excitement, had forgotten the gray hat. He wore the helmet, that talisman presented to him in Joy's native state. Halfway down he stopped on a ledge, uncoiling a long piece of rope he had brought with him from the plane. When he had it secured to a niche in the sheer wall, he absently shifted his .45 from his pocket to his belt. The gesture was not missed by Joy and she began to stare up and down the canyon floor below them as though expecting all sorts of horrible things to leap forth.

He fastened the rope carefully about her slim waist. "Hang on," he commanded and began to lower her over sixty feet of space. Swinging there, going slowly down, Joy saw the wing of the plane over them like the protecting hand of a saint.

"How . . . how will we get back up?" she called.

He fastened the rope carefully about her slim waist.
"Hang on," he commanded and began to lower
her over sixty feet of space.

"I'll manage it," Kurt promised.

She came to rest on a ledge below and Kurt came down like a descending bomb. When he had dropped beside her he released the rope from his grasp and let it hang. Fifty feet still remained between their ledge and the bottom, but the slope was not severe, and they had little difficulty in traversing it.

"What are we going to do now?" asked Joy.

Kurt produced the sharp pointed sample pick from his belt. "A ledge such as the one Nathan Reid must have found here is certain to be in evidence. We'll scout some of these ravines."

He had added the gold pan to his equipment for testing the wandering stream which brawled down through the ravine. His eyes held a far light and his mouth was set in a half smile which was more determination than humor.

"Later," said Kurt, "we'll visit the Maya city. I'd like to take a look at that big pyramid just for luck. I remember something about it from the journals. Gradually everything I read is coming back. Gee," he cried boyishly, "wouldn't it be swell to walk in on Kimmelmeyer before the eighth and slap an identical nugget on that desk of his!"

Some of his enthusiasm began to infect her. It was strange, this wish to defeat a dead man. At first the thought had been gruesome to her. But the dead man had hated Kurt Reid and something in that was helping her to understand, to want Kurt to succeed, to wish for victory for Kurt's sake.

They walked along the side of the brook, parting the small bushes which grew there, disturbing clouds of insects which rose angrily like hostile fleets of planes to jab sharp stingers into their fair skins.

Kurt stopped from time to time, taking up dirt from the creek and placing it in the big flat metal pan. He washed it with a swinging, rotating motion, picking out the larger rocks, doing his work carefully until only a little black sand remained in the bottom. Sometimes the sand contained flecks of bright yellow gold.

"See that color!" cried Kurt each time. "There's a vein along here, up above here. See there's more this time than there was last. We're getting closer and closer!"

Late in the afternoon, having dined upon a pocketful of raisins and a flinty biscuit apiece, they came upon the source of the creek. They were not far from the plane as they had not progressed swiftly, but it seemed a long way to Joy.

Suddenly Kurt gave a shout. He was pointing up at a streak of white rock. "Ore! That's gold up there!"

He scrambled ahead without watching his footing. Forgotten was his wound. He mounted high above Joy and began to hammer at the white quartz.

Then he stopped and came down. His face was so melancholy that Joy laughed at him.

"That's not it," said Kurt. "That's white quartz. Gold ore, yes, but I've got to get a piece with rose quartz in it. Come on, we're going back to the plane. Tomorrow's another day."

Tiredly she followed him through the approaching dusk. The brook was their trail part of the time and they slogged along, silent again, hemmed in by space and the depressing quietness of the place.

Kurt stopped so quickly that Joy bumped into his back. A sound had come up to them. The crackling of brush. The whisper of voices. A chilly fear ran through Joy like a rapier. She was unable to breathe, sensing danger, not from the sound but from Kurt's alert posture, from the quiver of his thin nostrils as though he could scent the air and discover the danger as cave men had discovered danger a million years before them.

Joy felt her heart swelling up, pounding inside her breast like a hammer, suffocating her.

Again the sound reached them, closer now. Two men with coppery skins emerged from the brush ahead, walking with their gaze on the ground as though reading a message there. They were trackers. Mayans!

Kurt did not move. The man in the lead, his black hair drawn down tight with a metal band, stopped, also sensing danger. His black eyes reached up, caught sight of Kurt and stared. The man's companion bumped him and glanced across the small clearing.

A yell more shrill than anything Joy had ever heard before rasped through the air. A cry of warning from the second Indian.

The first darted into the bushes, pulling an arrow from his quiver. Kurt heard the whistle of the feathered shaft. He drew the Colt .45 as though he were on a target range.

Flame ripped across the thick dusk. The Indian screamed and fell forward. His companion was running swiftly away. Kurt, unwilling to shoot a man in the back, let him go.

Joy's throat pulsed. She moaned a little, leaning heavily against Kurt, trying not to look at the last agonies of the dying man.

The brush was suddenly filled with cries and the crash of broken bushes. There were others, many others coming toward the sound of alarm and the shot. Kurt backed up, pushing Joy along with him. He looked anxiously about him for a barricade, something behind which they could hide and defend themselves. He found nothing.

"Run," he said and his voice was harsh.

"And . . . and leave you?"

"Run! I can't. My leg won't let me. If you get free, if they can't find you, then you can take the plane and perhaps help me. Go quickly. Damn it, run!"

Joy saw the logic behind the order. She did not question the rightfulness of it. Every instinct made her want to stay with Kurt but he had ordered her to do a thing and somehow he was not to be questioned.

In an instant she was gone. Kurt turned about and faced the clearing again. Men were pouring up through the trees, dimly seen except for the flashes of copper skin. The Mayans stopped when they came to the clearing edge. Kurt was waiting for them, waiting for them to make the first aggressive move.

A copper-tipped spear carved air in a flash of brilliance against the leaden hue of the dusk. When it struck a tree behind Kurt its shaft hummed.

An arrow sang shrilly in his ear and then an avalanche of feathered color came at him. Despair welled inside him. The .45 rapped again and again. Sparks streaked out far before him. Men thrashed about in the underbrush.

One clip gone, Kurt hastily began to load. But they would not grant him time for that. Like yellow-skinned tigers they ran across the intervening space, yowling and brandishing war clubs.

"Run! I can't. My leg won't let me. If you get free, if they can't find you, then you can take the plane and perhaps help me. Go quickly. Damn it, run!"

No time to reload. The sample pick was in Kurt's belt. He whipped it out. Its hand was a foot and a half long. One end of it was a hammer, the other was a wicked sharp point. Let them come.

The attack of the first man knocked Kurt back with its violence. The sample pick buried its point in the Indian's skull, coming away dripping.

The pack closed in. Kurt was borne to earth under a writhing blanket of unwashed greasy bodies. Hard edges hammered him. Nails tore at him. He fought back as best he could using every hold he knew.

But the end was certain, there before Kurt knew it. They held him inert under them, gripping his arms, punching him to see if he were dead. Then convinced that he was only half unconscious they dragged him along over the ground as though he were a sack of maize.

The grass was turned red as he passed, but through his half-closed eyes he saw five men who would never move again. He had paid his score in full.

They had forgotten Joy, perhaps. He could not see. The trail was long and when he reached the end of it he was slumped like an empty burlap bag.

Nathan Reid had known the trap he had set. Perhaps Nathan Reid's restless ghost was somewhere about, smiling with that cruel thin smile with which he had taken a rabble army to its death.

CHAPTER NINE

HOW long he had been there he did not know. Many dawns had come and gone. Many hot afternoons had passed by, melting into the cool of evening.

Fever hits hard on the heels of physical injury and the wounds were almost healed before Kurt Reid lost the lethargy of delirium and high temperature.

One day he sat up with a start, knowing where he was and why he was there, remembering Nathan Reid and Bruce and the Mayans. It was like awaking from a bad dream to find that it was so after all.

He was in an oblong room built of dirty limestone. The ceiling came together above him in steps, its architecture that of the Later Mayan Empire because of its false arch. The Mayans had never learned to make an arch.

Dried lake reeds went to make his hard bed. A square window, a mere hole in the thick rock walls, showed a section of blue sky and the drifting segment of a white cloud. The place was silent save for the drone of flies in the room.

Ten minutes of sitting up made him realize how weak he was. He lay back with a weary sigh, looking up at the smoky, stepped ceiling.

How in the name of God had he gotten there? Where was he? Why was he still alive?

That last fact made him wonder the most. It did not seem reasonable that he would be attacked, that he could kill five and still live himself. Something was wrong. And then when he thought about it hard a tugging thought made him shiver.

Were they keeping him for some terrible purpose?

He slept after that and dreamed of shifting horrors, of flames and pain and death.

The next day he was awakened by the entrance of an aged woman. She was fat and greasy. Her hair was braided and she was dressed in a dirty white cotton singlet. When she saw that he was conscious she stood staring at him a long time. Then she went out and returned with a copper bowl filled with maize and a heavy bread. Her study was disconcerting—she looked at him as one looks at a pig before slaughtering time.

Kurt sat up again. He was suddenly possessed with a restless warning, a nervousness. It was as though a dynamo had started up inside him, filling him with tingling electricity. How many days had passed? How close was it to the eighth of October? He was due back in New York. Otherwise Nathan Reid would win after all.

And what had happened to Joy? Had she gone with the ship? And where were Bruce and Sloan and Connelly?

He ate the maize with the ravenous appetite of past fever. When he had scraped the shining copper bowl of all it had held he found that its smooth bottom was a perfect mirror. A gaunt yellow face stared back at him. The eyes were sunken, a stubble of black beard had come out on his chin.

From the length of the beard he knew that he had been

there many, many days. Weeks perhaps. Why had they kept him?

His helmet had gone, his pockets were empty. The remains of bandages clung loosely to his arms and shoulders. He did not recognize his own identity. He was filled with the strange idea that it was not Kurt Reid.

And then voices drifted to him from the front of the hut. Men were speaking in Spanish out there. And one voice had the guttural American intonation he would have recognized anyplace.

Bruce!

The other man spoke slowly and clearly as though he were very old. "Now that the black devil is again awake, you are forced to wait no longer. You may be rewarded for bringing him here to us by witnessing his death. Perhaps we shall find other ways of rewarding you."

"The more speed the better," replied Bruce. "I'm sick of hanging around this place. I've done you a favor, now you can do one for me by speeding it up. To me, time is valuable."

"But how well I understand. However, there is such a thing as decorum. In the light of the full moon the rites shall be carried out. We have waited too long for this to be in a hurry."

"Waited too long?" said Bruce.

"How not? Perhaps fifty years. I myself scarcely remember the time. But I remember his face. He has not changed, he cannot age. Until he is devoured by flame, he will return twice each century to take his toll of our people. He is an avenging spirit and it is necessary that we kill him."

"Oh, certainly," agreed Bruce. "He's the one all right. What did he do the time before?"

"He came with a dozen men, all of them wild of eye and armed with weapons we thought strange and godlike. At first we accepted him, but when we refused to give what he wanted, he killed like a wolf that knows no satiation. We slaughtered the twelve, but him we could not kill. Perhaps our gods were against it, who knows?"

"He's the one," said Bruce. "I came far to tell you and to bring him to you. Perhaps I shall want a reward a little more definite than witnessing his death."

"Your service has been great. The three of you shall not want of our goods."

The voices faded away, still talking, leaving Kurt in the grip of a cold sweat. His staring eyes were filled with the knowledge of the Mayans' error.

He knew now why Nathan Reid had made him come down here. He looked a little like Nathan. Generally, anyway. Black hair, dark eyes, stringy figure. He had come booted, with a gun flaming in his hand.

They had known Nathan Reid would come back and Nathan Reid had sent him. They had waited for fifty years! The gruesomeness of such patience made Kurt shiver.

Nathan Reid had sent him into a trap and Bruce had clinched it. But how did Bruce tie up with all this?

He slept again and when he awoke it was late afternoon. The sun was on the wrong side of the building and it was very dark within. But in spite of the darkness, a square of light danced restlessly on the ceiling.

Kurt studied the square. It went back and forth, back and forth, sometimes quickly, sometimes slowly. Someone was carrying something shiny outside. In a moment the light would stop.

But the light did not stop. It went on and on for minutes. Curiosity made Kurt arise. He stumbled to the window and supported himself on the narrow ledge with his elbows, looking out.

The source of the light came from a small hut across a shallow ravine. It flashed with varying length.

Then Kurt knew exactly what it was. Talking sunlight! Heliograph! Coming from a window, using international Morse code.

Dash, dash, dot, dash. Dot, dot, dot. Dash.

That would be QST. "Calling, calling."

Flash, flash, flip, flash. Flip, flip, flip. Flash. "Calling."

For a moment Kurt was puzzled. Who would want to get in touch with him? Who would be here besides Bruce and Connelly and Sloan?

Joy!

It was like a shower of ice water. Kurt looked back at the room and saw the bright pan. It would be impossible to signal. He had no sunlight in his direction. He was forced to stand there and watch, powerless to answer.

He did not sleep well that night. With returning strength he was growing restless. No one of his vitality could remain down so very long. He awoke just as the sky was graying. He spent an hour trying to clean himself up, using the copper bucket of water which had been left inside the hut. It was a painful task, ridding himself of that stubbly chin growth, but he managed it.

He took off the now useless bandages and bathed himself. He felt better after that, almost well again.

When the sun came swinging out of the horizon he began the construction of a heliograph. He took the morning bread and placed it on the sill. Then he notched it with sights like those of a rifle. Finally he sunk the copper plate into the far end, making a hole in its center so that he could direct the beam with his improvised sight.

He tried his QST several times that morning and he began to be tormented by the fear that Joy had been taken away. Then at noon he received an answer.

Flip, flip, flip, flip. Flip. Dot, dash, dot, dot. Dot, dash, dot, dot. Dash, dash, dash. "HELLO," said Joy.

Kurt applied himself to his heliograph. "How did you get here?"

"They found me and brought me in."

"What are they going to do with you?" demanded Kurt.

"Nothing that I can see. They treat me with every courtesy but they won't let me walk outside."

Two stabs of sunlight flashing across the ravine. A silent conversation which went unnoticed by the village.

"Bruce is here."

"I know. He landed days ago," said Joy.

"Won't they do anything to him?"

"I guess not. They let him wander through the town without a guard. I can see the transport plane down on the strip of beach."

For an hour they talked on and then footsteps sounded outside Kurt's door and he was forced to hide his crude instrument.

The door opened and Bruce thrust his face inside. Bruce was tattered and unwashed. He had not shaved and even his glasses were smudged. Behind him stood an old man and two young warriors leaning on their copper-tipped spears. In that glimpse of the outside, Kurt saw the pyramid.

The old man with Bruce was dressed in a flowing robe. His eyes were steady and serene, his face was wrinkled and wise, but there was about him a certain streak of savageness which Kurt could feel rather than see.

"Hello, wise guy," said Bruce. "How are you getting on? Enjoying yourself, I hear."

Kurt looked steadily at him without answering.

"We came in just in time," said Bruce. "The natives were discussing whether or not you could be Nathan Reid. So we stood up for you. Yes, sir, we stood up for you. We said you were Nathan Reid. We said we was after you but that as a special favor we'd let them have the fun of killing you."

"Thanks," said Kurt, hands in his pockets, eyes very dark.

"It's a laugh on you," continued Bruce. "Your granddaddy raised hell down here, and you look enough like him to stir up their memories. They been waiting for this for fifty years. How do you like that?"

"Fine," said Kurt. "Fine."

"And they're setting up all the pins in the alley," said Bruce, rocking on his heels, overflowing with triumph. "You're an easy mark. You're dumb. You was a pushover, big boy. A

pushover. And now besides a good chunk of pay, the three of us are going to collect some lucre in the form of gold."

"Had all this planned, did you?" said Kurt. There was something in his voice like the mutter of distant thunder.

"Sure we did. And you fell for it. Old Kimmelmeyer was sweating for a while. He was scared you'd have dough enough to come down here by yourself."

"Kimmelmeyer behind this?"

"Sure he is. He hired us three to bring you down here. He put that ad in the *Eastern Pilot* himself and made sure you saw it. You don't think a shyster like Kimmelmeyer would pass up four millions and property, do you? Not on your life. He's got it all fixed. Old Nathan Reid didn't leave a good will. He let Kimmelmeyer draw it up. And now Kimmelmeyer can take the works himself without a squawk. 'Course he's going to be mighty surprised when we start the old bleed on him, but he'll still have plenty."

"So he wanted to make sure I'd die down here," said Kurt.

"Sure. We were going to just plain kill you after we found your granddaddy's gold, but this is better. I don't like straight murder."

"Of course you've got your scruples," replied Kurt.

"Oh, sure. And I'm going to get the *dinero* without having to bump you off. *Diga*," he said to the old man, reverting to Spanish, "tell him."

The old man's eyes lit up with a gleam of pleasure. "Tonight, devil though you are, you are going to die by fire. Prepare yourself, exhort your gods. They can do nothing for you

STORIES from the GOLDEN AGE

© 2012 Galaxy Press, LLC All Rights Reserved. Pulp magazines cover artwork is reprinted with permission from Argosy Communications, Inc.; Penny Publications, LLC; Hachette Filipacchi Media; and Condé Nast Publications.

FREE SHIPPING!
NO PURCHASE REQUIRED

☐ Yes, I would like to receive my **FREE CATALOG** featuring all 80 volumes of the *Stories from the Golden Age Collection and more!*

Name

Shipping Address

City   State   ZIP

Telephone   E-mail

Check other genres you are interested in: ☐ SciFi/Fantasy ☐ Western ☐ Mystery

6 Books • 8 Stories
Illustrations • Glossaries

6 Audiobooks • 12 CDs
8 Stories • Full color 40-page booklet

- -
Fold on line and tape

IF YOU ENJOYED READING THIS BOOK, GET THE ACTION/ADVENTURE COLLECTION **AND** SAVE 25%

BOOK SET	AUDIOBOOK SET
~~$59.50~~ $45.00	~~$77.50~~ $58.00
ISBN: 978-1-61986-089-6	ISBN: 978-1-61986-090-2

☐ Check here if shipping address is same as billing.

Name

Billing Address

City   State   ZIP

Telephone   E-mail

Credit/Debit Card #: _____

Card ID # (last 3 or 4 digits): _____

Exp Date: _____/_____ Date (month/day/year): _____/_____/_____

Order Total *(CA and FL residents add sales tax)*: _____

To order online, go to: **www.GoldenAgeStories.com** or call toll-free **1-877-8GALAXY** or 1-323-466-7815

NO POSTAGE
NECESSARY
IF MAILED
IN THE
UNITED STATES

BUSINESS REPLY MAIL
FIRST-CLASS MAIL   PERMIT NO. 75738   LOS ANGELES CA

POSTAGE WILL BE PAID BY ADDRESSEE

GALAXY PRESS
7051 HOLLYWOOD BLVD
LOS ANGELES CA   90028-9771

STORIES from the GOLDEN AGE
by L. Ron Hubbard

COLLECT THEM ALL!

GALAXY PRESS

7051 Hollywood Blvd., Suite 200 • Hollywood, CA 90028
1-877-8GALAXY or 1-323-466-7815
To sign up online, go to:
www.GoldenAgeStories.com

Prices set in US dollars only. Non-US residents, please call 1-323-466-7815 for pricing information or go to www.GoldenAgeStories.com.
Sales tax where applicable. Terms, prices and conditions subject to change.

3

against ours. Before you came for gold. Before you came for gold with fire.

"Now you're going to get gold!"

The Old One hitched his robe about him and went out. Bruce, with a lopsided smile, followed him.

Kurt sank down on the edge of the straw bed and stared at the wall.

Nathan Reid had taken another trick.

CHAPTER TEN

THE pungent odor of woodsmoke drifted into the dark room shortly after darkness had fallen. Kurt sniffed at it uneasily. He felt very like a trapped animal, unable to do anything about his circumstances. His strength, in this emergency, had returned to him.

He stopped in his pacing at the window. A fire was somewhere in the front of the building. He could see its reflected glare on the houses opposite the window. The black night was drawn down tight as a net over the village.

The wish to defeat Nathan Reid had carried him to this. But then, if he hadn't tried, he never would have met Joy. That seemed very vital to him and he felt himself standing in fear of the fact that he would have missed being with her.

What would happen to her now? She was dangerous to Bruce and therefore Bruce could hardly be expected to take her away. She was certainly no use to these Indians and they would therefore kill her as they were going to kill him.

He thought about her a little while. Her blue eyes, laughing. Her hair with its golden lights. Joy hadn't been afraid.

If only he could get to his plane somehow. But then, of course, they'd found the yellow ship. It wouldn't be there anymore.

His musings were interrupted by the sounds of men outside. The door was flung back. Straight Mayans were standing there, led by the old man in the robe. Their glistening bodies were silhouetted against the fires on top of the huge pyramid.

Kurt began to understand now. He'd come for gold, he was going to get gold.

He stepped out into the center of the military file. Coppery spears, coppery skins. Dark eyes which did not even look at him. These Mayans had remembered something of their ancient mercenaries, the Toltecs. They marched on either side of him, in two lines, in step.

The pyramid looked bigger than it was in the flaring light of the smoking fires at its top. Kurt became aware of a horde of people standing about the front of the base. Faces were turned exultantly, wonderingly, cruelly, in his direction.

This show was for the devil who had returned after fifty years. For the killer who had come for gold. And now they were going to give him the gold he wanted. They were going to give him death besides in spite of his charmed existence and his talisman.

Kurt held his head erect, neither looking to the left or right. He wouldn't give them the pleasure of seeing that he was afraid anyway. He marched like the soldiers and their copper spears. His boots rang above the sounds of bare feet on the stone pavements.

They reached the base of the pyramid. A ripple of sound went over the assembly like a wave. It died as Kurt started the ascent toward the narrow top.

The moon was shining now, clear and yellow, sparkling on

the surface of the lake. Great stone statues stood out in all their grotesque hideousness.

A shaft of memory came to Kurt's aid. Nathan Reid had described all this. A reversion from Christianity, a throwback to the savage paganism of their ancestors. The last grasp of a people to its past glory.

This was the temple of Kukulcán—a god who was represented by a man with bird and snake attributes. The great feathered serpent of the Aztec and the Toltec had originally been this Kukulcán. Mexican influence had brought in sacrifice, even cannibalism insofar as the witnesses of the rites were oftentimes required to partake of the flesh of the victim.

Kurt Reid, as he went up the stairway on the front of the pyramid, was climbing back through centuries to a decayed and warped survival of the cruelest religious customs. As he came closer to the top he saw that fires had been built all about the square blocks above—had been built in a rectangle which enclosed the images of deities.

At first it was apparent that no opening had been left in the flames and then he saw that the two front lines were at variant depth so that a man could turn from his course and go through unscathed. This was part of the magic mummery with which the priests held their restless people.

Passing between the scorching fires, Kurt first saw the image of the death god. It was a repulsive thing, this fancied likeness of death. It was a great stone skull with grinning teeth and clasped bony hands. Under it was seated a man incredibly like the stone image. The priest of death seemed to be drugged as he did not look up when Kurt entered the square.

And then Kurt received a shock. The carved stone image of Kukulcán had been done in such a way that it left a seat between the two outstretched, clawlike hands. And on that seat, arrayed in a feathered robe, sat Joy.

She did not look down. She stared straight ahead, unblinking. No motion of her lips or hands was apparent. She was obviously under the influence of some drug, thought Kurt.

God, what a fate to leave her to. Her golden hair had done the trick. Bruce had not wanted to identify himself with her and he had let the Mayans draw their own conclusions. The priests had not been slow in recognizing her potentialities. She would be held there, living embodiment of the sun until she died—or was killed because her usefulness was ended. True, she would be inviolate. No man would dare touch her. Such had been the reaction of the Mayans to the first blond white woman they had ever seen.

The men with the spears distributed themselves about the square, their shining backs to the fire, their eyes impassive. Kurt felt his arms grasped from behind.

The Ancient One approached, muttering a chant. He addressed Kurt in Spanish. "You came again. The Mayans are a hospitable people. You shall have your gold." He chanted again and then said, "So many warriors have you killed, so much damage have you done. So have you changed the seasons and blighted our crops. Your deviltry has brought plagues and famine. You are responsible for all we have suffered for fifty years.

"Now you are offered to Kukulcán, god of the sun, god of the sun metal, gold. Your own magic can avail you nothing against his, for he has sent a powerful servant down from the skies to help us." He pointed dramatically to Joy.

She did not move. She was holding the heavy staff of the feathered serpent stiffly upright beside her. Her robe was shining, made of golden feathers of tropic birds. Her blond hair curled down near her shoulders, sparkling in the light.

Kurt saw her bewitched stare and mourned that she would not give him just one sign. It would have made it easier for him.

He let his gaze roam about. Through the fires he could see the vague outline of the big plane on the beach. Bruce was somewhere in the crowd with Connelly and Sloan.

A crude metal crane was erected over a makeshift forge. These people had worked in metal years before the Spaniards came. From the crane was suspended a pot. A man was working at the bellows. The contents of the cauldron were bubbling and hissing.

Molten gold! Liquid fire! One thousand and sixty three degrees centigrade! Yes, they were going to give him gold.

He staggered back as though already feeling the sting of it. The men behind him held hard, muscles rippling on their naked backs.

Again Kurt looked at Joy. She was still staring straight before her, unmoving.

His eyes caught sight of something else. How could he have missed it before? The altar about the base of Kukulcán was made of gold, pure gold cemented together in irregular lumps. And in that gold were flecks of rose quartz.

She did not move. She was holding the heavy staff of the feathered serpent stiffly upright beside her. Her robe was shining, made of golden feathers of tropic birds.

My God, no wonder they hated Nathan Reid. He had stolen a part of their altar! A spot was empty near the tip, apparently chipped away. That would be the spot Nathan Reid had found that nugget Kimmelmeyer had balanced so carelessly in his hand.

So near to success and yet so far from it. The Ancient One was addressing the people below, flecks of foam on his lips as he spoke. A wild light was in his eyes. He was bringing something from the folds of his robe: Kurt's helmet with its goggles and its emblazoned dragon. They thought it was Kurt's idol. The Old One was mocking it, shaking it and making the goggles sparkle in the flames.

The Old One turned and came to Kurt. He jammed the helmet on Kurt's head with such ferocity that the goggles were shaken down until they covered Kurt's eyes.

The lenses gave him relief from the stinging, swirling smoke. The Old One had unconsciously done him a favor in mocking that poor Asiatic dragon.

The crane began to swing away from the fire now. It was precariously balanced, spilling some of its precious liquid on the stones where it spattered like beams of sunlight, exploding as it struck.

The men behind Kurt flexed their naked shoulders. They forced him to his knees. He was so near Joy he could have touched the skirt of her robe. Still she did not look at him.

The crane swung closer so that its heat scorched Kurt's face. The Old One and the ring of younger, naked priests were chanting in a high monotone, their breech clouts swinging back and forth as they gave up their bodies to the rhythm of the song.

My God, they were going to pour molten gold down his throat!

Kurt felt himself turn sick. He tried to struggle back to his feet and the hands closed hard about his arms, holding him. The crane swung nearer and nearer. In a matter of seconds he'd be dead!

Fascinated he watched the slow approach of the balanced cauldron. He tried to reach out with his booted foot and kick it away, but they prevented that. Even so, he touched the edge and spilled a full pint of the sizzling liquid.

He closed his eyes, gritting his teeth. The Old One was yelling more loudly. The crane was so fixed that a delicate mechanism could tip it without any actual physical touch.

The chant grew louder and louder, drowning the crackle of the flames.

How Nathan Reid's ghost must be laughing! How Bruce must be reveling in this. And Kimmelmeyer had sent him here, knowing all about it.

He resigned himself to his death before the hot breath of the cauldron. Joy was drugged, thought Kurt, that was well. She would not have to watch this.

Suddenly he caught a blur of motion. The chant broke. Men screamed and shrank quickly away. The feathered staff Joy had held came down in a blurred arc. Its heavy head struck the mechanism which tipped the cauldron.

A shower of flaming gold leaped up into the air. It came down instantly in a fine spray, scalding. Kurt cried out as drops struck his unprotected cheek. He felt his helmet scorch under the rain of flame. The lenses to his goggles were instantly bubbled where the gold had touched.

But the Mayans were almost naked. They wore no such protection as clothes and helmets and goggles. They screamed, some of them blinded forever. The rank odor of burning flesh was in the air. A crazed guard stumbled into the fire and was instantly a tower of flame, burning but still alive.

Kurt's mind acted swiftly. He was on his feet before all the gold had come down. He cried, "Come on, Joy!"

"Run to the plane!" she shouted, eyes alight. "I'll hinder you. Come back for me!"

Kurt knew that time would not allow an argument. He sprinted across the bodies toward the entrance. A swelling roar of the mob came up to him. Men were running up the steps on the front of the pyramid.

Flames were to the rear. Kurt knew it was either that or nothing. He seized a spear of a blinded guard. Men stood between him and the rear. He charged them. The spear bit deeply, snapped off. The target fell aside.

Kurt dived through the fire. Long steps were before him. He catapulted down them. The mob was streaming around the sides to intercept him. The jungle was still far away. He ran faster, each landing jarring his teeth.

A runner, faster than the others, was there waiting for him. Kurt sent the shaft of the spear before him like an arrow. It caught the Mayan in the forehead and drove him down. His body fell alongside Kurt's descent for several steps.

A gun flashed. That would be Bruce. Or Sloan or Connelly.

Kurt reached the bottom just ahead of the crowd. He ran toward the jungle edge, toward the place he had left the yellow plane, hoping against hope that the ship would still be there. Without it he could do nothing.

Shots sounded again, closer to him. He looked back into the mob, saw their open mouths, their angry eyes. He doubled his speed. He seemed tireless, exhilarated by the escape, bolstered up by his determination to lick Nathan Reid after all, driven onward by the necessity of pulling Joy out of the city.

He reached the edge of the jungle and flashed through the opening to a path. The moonlight was streaky before him, lighting his way.

CHAPTER ELEVEN

T HE restless pattern of the streaks of light was sufficient for Kurt's passage. Once in a while he checked his headlong run to dodge as some fancied ambush seemed to loom through the shadows.

Behind him the searching parties were spreading out, covering every conceivable trail. Once Kurt heard men running close behind him and he doubled his speed, placing as much distance between himself and his pursuers as possible.

After that he heard nothing. The silence should have made him easier, but it did not. He could fancy now that they were waiting silently for him at every turn of the path.

He came out into a clearing and saw the mountains there. In truth they were a gunsight, and he was instantly aware of his exact position. He had only to follow down, keeping that cleft in sight to arrive at the ravine where he had left the plane. If he could only be certain that the plane was still there!

Maybe they would kill the girl instantly for her treachery. All manner of doubts began to seep into Kurt's confidence, eventually shattering it.

For minutes he ran without stopping. Then he would pause and listen. On he would go, scanning the shadows. His boots made a terrific amount of noise on this soft turf—or so it seemed to him. Would he never reach that ravine?

He sprinted through a canopy of leaves, all in darkness for a moment. The bottom fell out from under him. He crashed down into the ravine. The drop was only ten feet but it jarred him. He stood up dizzily, faltering in his stride. Then he saw the gunsight again and his vigor returned.

He came to a fork in the trail. Two ravines met here to diverge again at a narrow angle. He was undecided and then chose the right-hand trail.

A flicker of light came from behind. He stopped and looked at it. The thing was bobbing up and down, back and forth. A man walking, carrying a torch. They were close on him again.

He began to run, avoiding the mighty boulders all about him. He was not quite sure which ridge held the plane. Nor was he certain that the plane was still there. Things looked different in the moonlight, but he had thought he could see the wing.

Shouts rose up far back of him. He stood clearly outlined in the moonlight, standing on barren white sand with the cliffs like gray ghosts on either side of him. Where was the rope he had left there?

The truth was slow in coming. He was in the wrong channel! He was one ravine up from the one he had climbed down. Nevertheless, if he could only scale this high cliff, he could get to the ship from the opposite side.

He had no rope, no sample pick to help him, but he started up. A fissure had been left in the porous rock, a chimney open at one side. By placing his back to one side and his feet against the other he was able to inch himself upward a little at a time. But the cliff was better than a hundred and fifty feet high and he saw too late that the chimney did not continue all the way.

A chorus of cries reached him. Torches bobbed like fireflies down the ravine. Men were coming up, running at full speed. They had found his trail, and in a moment they would discover him on the wall.

Kurt moved faster. He had to get himself out of the range of arrows and spears.

If Bruce or Sloan or Connelly were in that mob, he'd be shot down instantly.

Then they saw him. They stopped for a moment, lifting their torches up above their heads as though to shed their light higher. The moon was bright, sending ripples of light off their shoulders. The sparks from the torches fell unnoticed on bare backs.

With a bellowing concert of discovery, they closed in on the bottom of the cliff.

An arrow sang close by Kurt's hand. With a metallic ping it bent its copper point against the rock and fell back. Kurt went faster than before.

He had run miles already and he was tiring fast. He had forgotten his past sickness but he was remembering it now.

Just as his hands closed over the ledge thirty feet from the top, just as he left the chimney, the thought struck him that nothing prevented the Indians from climbing up the other side to get him.

And the wall above was sheer, too steep to climb. He needed a rope and he had none. He was trapped, unable to go either up or down.

Arrows were coming with greater regularity. He leaned back from the edge, watching the gleaming points pass up and turn back on themselves for a swift descent vertical.

An occasional arrow came over the edge with just enough momentum to fall at Kurt's feet. He picked up a handful. They wouldn't be able to shoot them again anyway.

And then Kurt was obsessed with a coldblooded thought. Those Mayans were used to climbing. Maybe he saw a way out of it.

Cupping his hands, his dark eyes glittering, he yelled, "*¡Ven aca! ¡Ven aca, carajos!* Come up and get me!"

A shrill chorus greeted the dare. Kurt, crouching on the ledge, his helmet straps flapping in the brisk wind, cried, "You yellow snails, *¡ven aca!*"

He did not show too much of his head. Bruce or Sloan or Connelly might be waiting down there for him.

A scratching sound reached him after a long silence. Sure enough the men were coming. Looking down the fissure of rock he could see their bronzed shoulders moving. There were three in a row.

Kurt's mouth tightened to a slit. He felt like laughing and knew how close he was to hysteria—as near as a man of Kurt's temperament can get.

"Come on!" he cried almost joyfully. "Come on and get me!"

The first in the line looked up with startled surprise at the nearness of the voice. Then he climbed faster. One hand clutched a knife between two fingers.

Kurt waited. When the Indian was within three feet of the top, Kurt very deliberately reached down and took the knife wrist in his powerful grasp. He pulled up. The Indian, surprised at such tactics, could do nothing but use the aid to his climbing.

Around the Mayan's shoulder was coiled a rope. The Mayans had been the first to so use sisal hemp, carrying rope everywhere with them. This fellow, to his own danger, was obeying the custom.

Kurt pulled until he could reach the rope with his free hand. Then he suddenly released his grasp. With a startled shout, the Mayan fell back, unable to keep his holds, leaving the hemp in Kurt's hands.

The two others in the chimney were knocked loose. Their screams rose in a terrified discord as they turned over and over through space. The thuds of their bodies striking the rocks below came dully up to Kurt.

Kurt lost no time. He had what he needed now. He tied the bundle of arrows together. They were heavy and strong, making a good weight. Then, like a sailor throwing a lead line to sound depth, he started to swing his rope back and forth along the cliff side.

Each time it swung, it gathered momentum, until it was reaching horizontal with every swing. At last he had it spinning in a mighty circle. He released his hold suddenly. The arrows shot upward. Kurt held his breath. The bundle landed between two big rocks. Cautiously he tested it. It held!

After that there was no stopping him. He went up the line like a human elevator. He reached out and snatched at the top, holding the edge, dragging himself further upward.

A shadow loomed over him, monstrous against the moon.

He saw something gleam an instant. He dodged, instinctively throwing himself to solid ground over the edge.

A bullet snapped close by his head. He sprang up. The twitching eyes of Connelly met his. Connelly had come up from the other side!

Kurt dived in for the gun. Connelly had hesitated for an instant and that instant had meant his death.

Kurt twisted the man about in a half circle. Grasping the gun, Kurt threw Connelly away from him. Connelly shrieked in terror. His feet fought to keep the edge. His grip, moistened by sweat, came loose from the gun.

Connelly plunged downward through a hundred and fifty feet, his cry cut off short as he struck.

The plane was sitting where he had left it. Kurt, with a shout, darted toward it. Other men were moving along the sandy ridge. They were briefly glimpsed.

Kurt reached the plane. Running feet were behind him. He whirled and took a quick aim with Connelly's gun. Without waiting to see whether he had hit his mark, he jumped into the cabin and reached for the throttles and booster.

The engine started with a blasting roar, making the ship quiver. Disregarding the perils of taking off with a cold engine, thrust beyond the reach of all caution, Kurt jammed the throttle all the way down and came about on the ground.

Men snatched at his wings. He shot twice from the cockpit. The ship was suddenly free. Fighting it to keep it on the narrow runway, he slammed along the sand, engine bellowing, wings fighting to take the air.

And then he was away and free. A man below was staring up with a white face, firing with an automatic.

Kurt, exhilarated and unafraid, leaned out over Bruce and disdainfully thumbed his nose.

CHAPTER TWELVE

THE lake was a sheet of beaten silver in the moonlight. High above it, traveling fast in his own element, Kurt could see the altar fires still smoldering on the pyramid. Now if nothing had happened to Joy . . .

The streak of white down there was the landing place the transport plane had used. The transport was still there, great wings spread unattended.

Without waiting to look the scene over, Kurt shot down for a fast landing. Sand flew up under his wheels. He cut the engine to idling speed as he coasted to a stop.

The village had been silent a moment before. Now it seemed that a thousand men came out of nowhere to run toward the plane. They came from the huts, from the pyramid, just as though they had been waiting for this move. The leaves of the trees blocked away the moonlight in spots, making the charging throng appear and disappear as though wafted onward by magic rather than human feet.

Kurt reached behind him. He knew what was there, knew how to use them. A light machine gun came up in his hands. He pulled back the loading handle and dropped to the ground. Let them try for him now. He was ready and waiting.

The first rank came within a hundred feet of him. He pulled the trigger. The belt began to eat through the breech.

A stream of hot sparks fled out from the muzzle, lighting up the sand for yards. The chattering howl of the gun was deafening.

The first rank melted, the second stopped. The gun raved on, eating its way through the Mayans with leaden teeth.

With a scream of terror the Indians fled. Kurt cradled the smoking hot gun under his arm and ran in the direction of the hut he knew had once contained Joy. He did not know that she would be there, but something magnetic was drawing him toward the spot.

Arrows whistled about him, but he paid them no heed. Once started he could not be stopped. He no longer felt vulnerable. If they had done anything to Joy he would clean up this ruined town as fire cleans an ant hill.

A voice was calling to him. Joy!

"Here I am! Here I am, Kurt!"

He sprinted on toward the hut. The door was closed, barred and locked with numerous barriers. Kurt beat his fists against them. "Coming, Joy."

But the barriers would not give way. Men were lining up on the beach, waiting for his return. He called out, "Get into the corner behind something. I'm going to shoot the door down!"

"Fire, Gridley!" cried Joy.

The machine gun chattered again. Splinters flew from the panels. Smoke wreathed up as the wood burned under the onslaught of sparks.

Kurt slammed his boot heel against it. It caved in. Joy

was suddenly there, gripping his arm, looking at him with starry eyes.

"I knew you'd come," she said.

Gone were the feathered robes. In their place she had put her own trim clothes, now torn. But she still carried the staff of the feathered serpent.

"They were going to kill you and me together when they found you," she said.

Kurt turned on the beach. He had had it in mind to destroy the transport plane. Now he saw that it was far away from the yellow ship. He did not dare wait that long.

He knew he had to get away. Already he might be too late in getting back to New York.

They ran down to the waiting, idling ship. Kurt stopped within a few feet of it. His way was blocked again. The light machine gun started up. The flashes of powder were so close together that they appeared like one great flare.

The Mayans scattered again. Kurt thrust Joy into the cabin and followed her. His machine gun was empty, and he tossed it in back. The plane came around with a blast from its hot exhaust stacks.

The Indians, brave again, tried to close upon it. A single pistol shot came out from under the wing of the transport ship.

Then the yellow plane was up and over the lake, beating the ground with the thunder of its motor.

"I should have destroyed their crate," shouted Kurt. "They'll follow us." Then he stared at Joy aghast. "My God, I forgot the gold nugget!"

Joy smiled. Her hand went into the pocket of her skirt and came forth holding a glinting, shining thing. "I thought," said Joy, "that you might be in a hurry when you came back and I brought a nugget with me. They didn't notice in all the fuss of your getting away."

The plane wobbled for a moment on its course and then, its attention no longer to be ignored, Kurt discontinued the kiss.

In the morning they landed at Progreso, scanning the skies behind them for pursuit.

The old Spaniard appeared magically on the beach, smiling, genuinely glad to see them again.

"I had thought you would never come back," he said.

"But we did," replied Kurt with a grin. "Please, *señor*, those others are behind us, following us. We must have gas and quickly."

"Gas it will be," said the Spaniard and went off to procure it.

A half-hour later, when the fluid was gurgling into the tanks, a low mutter came out of the south. Presently a speck could be seen just above the horizon. The transport plane.

"Quick," said Kurt, starting the motor and pressing a few bills upon the Spaniard at the same time. "What is the date?"

"The seventh . . . I think. *Puede ser* but that it is the eighth? *Si, yo creo* . . . The eighth, *señor*. The eighth it is!"

"The eighth," moaned Kurt. "And I have to be in New York before midnight tonight!"

"But it's only seven o'clock now," said Joy, hopefully. "That's nineteen hours. . . . Goodbye, *señor*."

The yellow plane lashed down the strip of sand and took

the air again. The Spaniard waved behind them and then jerked up his head at the sound of other motors in the sky. The transport plane was not stopping at Progreso. It would first see the finish of Kurt Reid.

Two shadows fled across the surface of the Caribbean. At first they were far apart and then gradually the distance began to close between them. The transport plane was miles an hour faster than the other and its light load of gas and equipment was even increasing the advantage.

Joy's glance was restless as she looked back. She saw the set of Kurt's mouth, saw the little drops of gold which had clung to the bizarre helmet. Each time she saw Kurt's eyes she dismissed her fears. They'd win out somehow.

She began to suspect that they should have stayed at Progreso, but then the time limit would not allow that. They were now far from land. While they had been in Progreso, Bruce could have tried nothing.

She could fancy his smudged glasses, his coarse mouth, his anger as he drove the transport plane after them. Sloan would be with him, his bulging eyes ready to squint down the sights of a machine gun.

Kurt turned back and looked. "They're gaining. Get that machine gun out. The loaded one."

Swallowing hard, Joy obeyed him. He let go the controls and she took them. A glow of happiness came over her. He trusted her, had confidence in her. Then she remembered the coming hail of lead and swallowed again.

"Bank and go back past them," ordered Kurt.

She put the ship about in a heart-stopping vertical, placing Kurt on the side next to the transport.

The big plane veered off, but not quickly enough. Kurt raised the machine gun, sighted at a spot in advance of the twin propellers and let drive.

Bruce dived out of range. Sloan's face was visible for an instant through an open window. Sloan had a dead pan, the same lack of expression he had used when he had first shot Kurt. His codfish mouth was working, he was talking to Bruce.

The yellow ship followed down. Suddenly the transport plane stabbed its props upward. White flame ripped out of a window. Fabric ripped away from the yellow wings. The slugs were taking effect.

Joy, trying to stay cool, let the yellow ship dive past. She heard Kurt's gun start up. Its incessant hammering seemed to obscure her vision. She caught a brief glimpse of the other ship. For an instant it was hanging on its props, about to stall out of the position, but while it was there it made an excellent target.

Kurt shouted. Joy saw flames. She banked again. They were down close to the waves now, flying almost with their wheels in the white caps.

The transport plane fell out of its stall. One wing was down and it curved away in a great arc. Joy saw the smoke it trailed behind it. Then she knew that it was hit. Hit and burning.

A man leaped through the swinging door. He had no chute. He went whirling through space like a bomb, striking the water long before the transport. Sloan.

Bruce rode the flaming coffin down. When it hit it seemed to explode. Steam shot skyward, mingled with spray.

After that there was nothing but scraps of floating wreckage. Joy circled as though unable to drag her eyes away from the sight.

Kurt shook the controls, took them and headed the plane toward the north. Joy, suddenly very weak from reaction, slumped back in her seat and wondered, for Kurt's sake, if they would be in time.

CHAPTER THIRTEEN

A T eleven-thirty that night, Kimmelmeyer prepared himself for bed. His immense bedroom was dwarfed by the four-poster he had purchased from an antique dealer and the carpet was very soft. The lights were subdued, but even then they reflected themselves upon his black-fringed pate.

Kimmelmeyer, dressed in purple pajamas, threw back the sheets and slid within. He lay there for some time without covering himself up. He gave himself over wholeheartedly to the dreams in which he had dared to indulge during the last month.

What would he do with Nathan Reid's millions? What wouldn't he do! Big cars, a bigger house, beautiful women.

Praise the day that crazy old fool had come into his office, sent by a legal friend. He had stamped up and down the room while dictating the conditions of his will. He had stamped and stormed and had loosed fragments of his wrath against the world at large.

He was Nathan Reid, thwarted in everything but the disgusting accumulation of money. And who did he have to leave the money to? No one. No one at all but a fool who had disobeyed him at every turn. A man who had made an aerial chauffeur out of himself instead of a military hero.

Son of his son, perhaps, but then Nathan Reid's son had not been so much in Nathan Reid's eyes. He had run away to Annapolis, that's what he had done, ungrateful pup. Joined the Navy just because he knew it would make his father mad. And the Navy? Damn the Navy. Hadn't they stolen Nicaragua from him?

Stamping and storming and damning the world at large. He wasn't going to leave his wealth to a disobedient pup. Not he! Let the yellow belly suffer some of the things Nathan Reid had suffered, let him go down and rot in the tropics. Good riddance. Let the name Reid die with Nathan.

Kimmelmeyer chuckled to himself and covered his fat body. Oh yes, he'd agreed with the old fool. He'd told him he was doing right. So Nathan Reid's legal advisors wouldn't hear of such a plan, eh? Well, the plan was perfectly just. Perfectly just. Yes, he'd draw the will. Glad to do it for the friend of a friend. Perfectly legal will.

And suppose this Kurt Reid came back with the ore?

Nathan Reid had laughed. That ore was part of a Mayan altar and the Mayan men were still there to guard it. The pup didn't have any chance of getting it. Let Kurt Reid have the directions if he wanted them. He wouldn't come back.

But suppose he did?

Then send the damned money to charity. Any charity. Those legal wolves of his wouldn't get it. Name any outfit that was reliable and the trick was done.

What? Was the job finished already? Fine. Splendid. That was capital! Very good work, Kimmelmeyer.

Again Kimmelmeyer smiled, squirming into a softer portion

of the mattress. The charity had been his own thought. He'd already handled their trustees. A few greased palms and everything was for Kimmelmeyer.

At this late hour, nothing could have slipped up. He should have received a radio from them. He'd wanted to know the instant Kurt Reid died. Too bad they couldn't have gotten a decent operator. A woman, they'd said, and Kurt had insisted. Oh, well, they'd probably had to kill her too. Some worthless tramp, no doubt.

How he'd spend those millions!

A soft footfall reached him. Was it possible that a servant was still awake at this hour? Kimmelmeyer turned on a lamp beside his bed. It threw shadows grotesquely upon the walls.

The door creaked, came open. Kimmelmeyer shrieked. He hunched himself back to the top of the bed as though trying to escape. He threw up his fat arm and hid his eyes.

The gaunt apparition must be a ghost, come back to haunt him. It could be nothing else. Kurt Reid was dead in the jungles of Yucatán!

And still the apparition advanced across the room. Another was following it. A smaller, slighter person with a merry light in her eyes.

"Get on a bathrobe," snapped Kurt.

Kimmelmeyer quivered like gelatin. "Where . . . where is Bruce . . . ?"

"Dead at the bottom of the Caribbean. Sloan's dead, Connelly's dead. It's twenty minutes to twelve. We've still got time to compare this ore. Where are the papers?"

"They . . . they're here, in my desk. . . . I . . ." Kimmelmeyer

99

was fighting to regain his poise. He mustn't let on the part he had played in this. He must put up a front. This Kurt Reid was real, altogether too real. Big and threatening.

"Don't kill him here," said Joy, maliciously. "I'd hate to see this rug all dirtied up." She winked at Kurt, trying to keep a straight face.

Kurt scowled like a thundercloud and his voice was like a thunderclap. "Get those papers!"

Kimmelmeyer, struggling into a purple robe, was quick to obey. He had everything right there, he said. Only a second. Only a second. He threw the legal sheets out on the desk, brought forth the nugget he had been hiding there.

Kurt placed his own piece of ore beside it. They matched perfectly.

"I hope . . . hope you'll remember everything I've done for you," choked Kimmelmeyer with a sick smile. "Here, sign this, and this and this. . . . But I need a witness."

"You'll do," said Kurt to Joy. "And ahoy outside there. Come on in."

A blue coat and brass buttons loomed through the entrance. It was the cop on the beat, his ruddy face very straight. "I guess, sor, that ye're not akidding me after all. I heard him ask for this feller Bruce, just like you told me to listen for."

"Good going. Have you got the warrant I swore out? Then present it after I've signed this and you've witnessed them."

The business was done in a matter of seconds. The officer witnessed the signature and the transaction with tongue twisted painfully between his lips.

Joy signed with a flourish. Everything was done now. A

court would place the stamp of approval upon it later, but they didn't have to wait for that.

Kimmelmeyer, shrinking away from the officer, was ordered to get into his clothes. Protesting, he was led away, out of the house and to the waiting police car. He would soon be standing trial for the unanswerable crime of attempted murder and attempted fraud.

Joy and Kurt went outside. Joy was gay, tired out but not willing to admit it even to herself.

"And thus it ends," she said, leaning on the staff of the feathered serpent.

Kurt looked at her for a moment and then frowned. That remark wasn't refusal, it was an invitation. He bounced the two nuggets in his hand and his smile broadened. "Ah, yes, thus it ends. By the way, do you prefer a plain gold band from this nugget or a fancy one from this?"

She saw that he meant it and stood close to him. A minute or so later they heard the taxi driver who had brought them say, "Where next, boss?"

"The town house," replied Kurt with a lordly air. "Ah, yes, the town house with all despatch."

"And jump a couple of red lights," said Joy, "I feel adventurous."

The taillight of the cab was lost down the dark street like the glowing end of a cigar butt . . . or perhaps the last embers of an altar fire in far-off Yucatán.

STORY PREVIEW

STORY PREVIEW

NOW that you've just ventured through one of the captivating tales in the Stories from the Golden Age collection by L. Ron Hubbard, turn the page and enjoy a preview of *Man-Killers of the Air*. Join Smoke Burnham, a colorful daredevil pilot who's gone broke creating a new fighter plane. With his principal financier hot on his tail to recoup his investment, Smoke enters an international race that will take him into the skies of Central America, over the Andes and across the Brazilian jungle—with only death as his copilot.

MAN-KILLERS
OF THE AIR

G IRARD was standing with both feet solidly planted, both hands shoved into the pockets of a pure camel's-hair overcoat. Girard's face looked as though someone had started to mold it from soggy putty and had then become bored with the job.

Girard was a big man—knew it, said it and acted it. He could afford to be a big man. He was one of the greatest newspaper publishers in the United States, one of the greatest exponents of that fourth stage of the newspaper, yellow journalism. He had once tipped a waiter a thousand-dollar bill, and the next day he had fired a legman for being twenty-five cents over on his swindle sheet.

Girard was surrounded by his own men, but one never saw those. They were dressed plainly, looked plain, were plain, and always nodded eagerly, "YES!"

"Well, well, well!" rumbled Girard. "That was some record, my boy, some record! Hey, you over there with the movie camera, want my picture shaking Burnham's hand?"

The movie man started to comply and then saw the look Smoke Burnham gave him. "No," said Smoke. "We aren't waving any flags. Not today. And I'm not shaking hands with you, Girard, any day!"

Girard was startled. "But, my boy—"

"Save it," said Smoke. "Let's get ahead with our business. You came up here to make me fork over the dough you lent me. And you've got the sheriff right there behind you, so don't deny it. You're foreclosing on Burnham Aeronautical Company, but you don't want to do it until the crowd goes."

Patty looked at Girard and licked her feline lips. Girard stared at both pilot and cheetah.

"Who put you wise?" he demanded.

"I did, mister. You haven't got a lease on all the brains in this country. You want this new fight-plane so you can turn it over to the government."

"But how—"

"I know what you're up to. You've got an air defense campaign underway, Girard. You're saying that the Japs are about to fly across San Francisco and wipe us out with bombers. And you're saying via a hundred newspapers that we haven't a single plane to withstand that offense.

"And, furthermore, you've challenged anyone to produce such a plane."

"You'd better watch out!" cried Girard, as though he wielded a saber instead of a Malacca cane.

"And," rapped Smoke, "you're going to foreclose on me, take the plans of this ship, the ship itself, and turn it over to the Army. That's patriotism! That's honor! You jump your ad rates on the resulting circulation and clean up."

Girard still waved the cane. He might have struck Smoke, because there were plenty of men behind Girard. But the cheetah was still licking her lips, and Smoke's hand was loose on the leash.

Two fighters, identical with the one Smoke had just flown in, crouched in the hangar. Smoke pointed to them. "Those two ships are company property. The one I used today belongs to Melanie King. I gave her the bill of sale. Now go ahead and serve your papers."

The sheriff, at Girard's nod, stepped up, skirting Patty's striking range. Although Patty had never struck anyone, people thought she did, and that was just as good.

Smoke began to smile and then to grin. The effect through the grime was ghastly, but he meant it.

"If you'll come inside," said Smoke, "I'll sign everything up and we'll all go have some lunch."

Girard's face was puzzled. Smoke Burnham had more records than Girard had newspapers. A story about Smoke was worth a hundred-thousand circulation jump. But that was no sign Smoke was an open book. Warily, Girard stepped into the hangar in Smoke's wake.

Smoke indicated some folding chairs at the back, "Sit yourself down, gentlemen. I haven't any cigars, but I see you've brought your own." He thrust a cigarette into his mouth at a climbing angle and lit up. Patty sat down in front of him, watching the curling blue wisps.

Girard, far from trusting Smoke, seated himself. It was all that he could do.

Smoke, still holding the burning match in spite of the mammoth sign: *No Smoking! Fire Hazard!* looked casually about him. Under the belly of the first pursuit ship there was a small puddle of gasoline, spilled at the last filling and not yet wholly evaporated.

109

Smoke flipped the burning match into the puddle.

A geyser of white flame shot up. A piece of cotton waste, soaked with oil, ignited with a crackling sound.

Girard jumped to his feet. "Fire! My God, *fire!*"

Smoke watched the flames engulf the shiny metal. A tongue slapped out and sideswiped the other ship. The heat rose from seventy to two hundred in a space of seconds.

Girard's crowd charged toward the hangar's doors, shrieking. Patty bared her fangs and unsheathed her claws in fear. Acrid fumes leaped, black and greasy.

On the outside of the hangar the crowd surged, shouting advice, shouting prayers, shouting anything as long as they made noise.

Alex ran wildly about crying, "Anybody seen Burnham? Where's Smoke?"

Newspaper men were milling, bellowing, "Where's Girard? Mr. Girard's in there!"

The thickening smoke was heavy and hot, completely filling the hangar. It was thick enough to carve.

A staggering man came out of the flame-seared maw. He was lugging another man.

Alex cried, "It's Smoke!"

The reporters yelled, "There's Girard!"

Smoke, stumbling and coughing, dropped his burden and then fell flat on his face. With a glance, Alex saw that Smoke was still all in one piece and that Girard was breathing.

Alex suddenly confronted the reporters. "There you are, boys! Get those pictures! Get this story! There you are!"

"What happened?" demanded a pale-faced newshawk.

Alex waved his hands majestically. "Girard accidentally threw a lighted cigar into a gasoline can and then Smoke stayed behind, searching for him. Looking through all that flaming hell. Fumbling under the ships, around already burning chairs. He heard a sound like coughing and crept nearer, not letting himself retreat from the searing, scorching heat. And then he found Girard. He found Girard, gentlemen, at the risk of his own life! And there's Girard, safe and sound. But he would be but a blackened corpse if Smoke Burnham had not—"

Girard was sitting up. He saw the reporters running toward the phones. It was too late to stop them. And besides, circulation would soar instantly with those headlines. Money was in the making.

But that did not keep Girard from rolling closer to Smoke. The publisher's flame-stung face was the color of raw beef. His eyes were a sickly red.

"You win, Burnham. But I'll make you a bet. I'll bet this place rebuilt against that one last pursuit plane."

Smoke grinned and lit a cigarette, as though he had not had enough smoke as it was. Patty, licking scorched fur, watched him with adoring eyes.

"Okay," said Smoke. "What's the bet?"

"That you can't win my transcontinental derby next month."

Smoke nodded. "Do you recall the other contest before that?"

"Yes. You'll have to win that before you can get into the derby."

"Make it a place twice as big as this and you're on."
Girard smiled, circulation figures dancing before his eyes.
"All right, Burnham. We'll have that put on paper."

To find out more about *Man-Killers of the Air* and how you can
obtain your copy, go to www.goldenagestories.com.

GLOSSARY

GLOSSARY

STORIES FROM THE GOLDEN AGE *reflect the words and expressions used in the 1930s and 1940s, adding unique flavor and authenticity to the tales. While a character's speech may often reflect regional origins, it also can convey attitudes common in the day. So that readers can better grasp such cultural and historical terms, uncommon words or expressions of the era, the following glossary has been provided.*

---

altimeter: a gauge that measures altitude.

Annapolis: the capital of Maryland and the site of the US Naval Academy, founded in 1845.

beam: an early form of radio navigation using beacons to define navigational airways. A pilot flew for 100 miles guided by the beacon behind him and then tuned in the beacon ahead for the next 100 miles. The beacons transmitted two Morse code signals, the letter "A" and the letter "N." When the aircraft was centered on the airway, these two signals merged into a steady, monotonous tone. If the aircraft drifted off course to one side, the Morse code for the letter "A" could be faintly heard. Straying to the opposite side produced the "N" Morse code signal.

cabin job: an airplane that has an enclosed section where passengers can sit or cargo is stored.

Colt .45: a .45-caliber automatic pistol manufactured by the Colt Firearms Company of Hartford, Connecticut. Colt was founded in 1847 by Samuel Colt (1814–1862), who revolutionized the firearms industry.

conquistador: a Spanish conqueror or adventurer.

cowl: a removable metal covering for an engine, especially an aircraft engine.

crate: an airplane.

El: elevated railway.

filibustero: (Spanish) filibuster; this term derived from the Spanish *filibustero* for "pirate," "buccaneer" or "freebooter," individuals who attack foreign lands or interests for financial gain without authority from their own government. It applied to Anglo-American adventurers in the mid-nineteenth century who tried to take control of various Caribbean, Mexican and Central American territories by force of arms.

fire, Gridley: refers to Charles Vernon Gridley (1844–1898); US naval officer who started the Battle of Manila Bay in the Spanish-American War with the order from his commanding officer, "You may fire when you are ready, Gridley." The Spanish fleet was annihilated without the loss of a single American life. This dramatic victory eventually led to the US annexation of the Philippines.

G-men: government men; agents of the Federal Bureau of Investigation.

great seal: the principal seal of a government or state, with which official documents are stamped.

heliograph: a device for signaling by means of a movable mirror that reflects beams of light, especially sunlight, to a distance.

henequen: a plant that has large thick fibrous leaves shaped like swords, the fiber from which is used in making rope and twine. Native to tropical America, chiefly the Yucatán Peninsula of Mexico.

hoodoo: one that brings bad luck.

huckster: a street peddler.

jewelry rock: gold-bearing vein quartz.

Jonah: somebody who brings bad luck.

key: a hand-operated device used to transmit Morse code messages.

kiting: flying.

knickerbockered: clothed in loose-fitting pants gathered at the knee or calf.

Lake Pontchartrain: a lake in southeastern Louisiana north of New Orleans.

Leavenworth: Fort Leavenworth; the site of a federal penitentiary in Kansas.

legman: a reporter who gathers information by visiting news sources, or by being present at news events.

Malacca: the stem of a species of palm, brown in color and often mottled, used for making canes and umbrella handles; named after a town in western Malaysia.

monoplane: an airplane with one sustaining surface or one set of wings.

mouthpiece: a lawyer, especially a criminal lawyer.

mufti: civilian clothes; ordinary clothes worn by somebody who usually wears a uniform.

mummery: a pretentious or hypocritical show or ceremony.

newshawk: a newspaper reporter, especially one who is energetic and aggressive.

patois: a regional form of a language, especially of French, differing from the standard, literary form of the language.

peg-topped: describing pants that are full and gathered at the hips and narrow at the ankles.

puede ser: (Spanish) could be.

QST: radio signal meaning "general call to all stations." The Q code is a standardized collection of three-letter message encodings, all starting with the letter "Q"; initially developed for commercial radiotelegraph communication and later adopted by other radio services.

rudders: devices used to steer aircraft. A rudder is a flat plane or sheet of material attached with hinges to the craft's stern or tail. In typical aircraft, pedals operate rudders via mechanical linkages.

sap: blackjack; a short, leather-covered club, consisting of a heavy head on a flexible handle, used as a weapon.

Scheherazade: the female narrator of *The Arabian Nights,* who during one thousand and one adventurous nights saved her life by entertaining her husband, the king, with stories.

sideslip: (of an aircraft when excessively banked) to slide sideways, toward the center of the curve described in turning.

sisal: a strong fiber obtained from the leaves of a plant native to southern Mexico and now cultivated throughout the tropics, used for making rope, sacking, insulation, etc.

soup: a thick fog.

spatted wheels: a structure around the top of the wheels of a fixed airplane landing gear.

sub-Thompson: a type of machine gun that fires short pistol rounds, named after its creator, John Taliaferro Thompson, who produced the first model in 1919.

TAT: Transcontinental Air Transport, airline founded in 1928. It was one of the first to be geared to passenger service at a time when most airlines focused on air mail. In 1930, it merged with Western Air Express to form what became TWA.

three-point: three-point landing; an airplane landing in which the two main wheels and the nose wheel all touch the ground simultaneously.

Toltecs: members of an Indian people living in central Mexico before the advent of the Aztecs and traditionally credited with laying the foundation of Aztec culture.

uppers, on my: on one's uppers; poor; in reduced circumstances. First recorded in 1886, this term alludes to having worn out the soles of one's shoes so badly that only the top portions remain.

wig-wag: a method of using flags or pennants to send signals.

wing collar: a shirt collar, used especially in men's formal clothing, in which the front edges are folded down in such a way as to resemble a pair of wings.

yo creo: (Spanish) I believe.

Yucatán: a peninsula mostly in southeastern Mexico between the Caribbean Sea and the Gulf of Mexico.

L. Ron Hubbard
in the Golden Age
of Pulp Fiction

*In writing an adventure story
a writer has to know that he is adventuring
for a lot of people who cannot.
The writer has to take them here and there
about the globe and show them
excitement and love and realism.
As long as that writer is living the part of an
adventurer when he is hammering
the keys, he is succeeding with his story.*

*Adventuring is a state of mind.
If you adventure through life, you have a
good chance to be a success on paper.*

*Adventure doesn't mean globe-trotting,
exactly, and it doesn't mean great deeds.
Adventuring is like art.
You have to live it to make it real.*

—*L. Ron Hubbard*

L. Ron Hubbard
and American
Pulp Fiction

B ORN March 13, 1911, L. Ron Hubbard lived a life at least as expansive as the stories with which he enthralled a hundred million readers through a fifty-year career.

Originally hailing from Tilden, Nebraska, he spent his formative years in a classically rugged Montana, replete with the cowpunchers, lawmen and desperadoes who would later people his Wild West adventures. And lest anyone imagine those adventures were drawn from vicarious experience, he was not only breaking broncs at a tender age, he was also among the few whites ever admitted into Blackfoot society as a bona fide blood brother. While if only to round out an otherwise rough and tumble youth, his mother was that rarity of her time—a thoroughly educated woman—who introduced her son to the classics of Occidental literature even before his seventh birthday.

But as any dedicated L. Ron Hubbard reader will attest, his world extended far beyond Montana. In point of fact, and as the son of a United States naval officer, by the age of eighteen he had traveled over a quarter of a million miles. Included therein were three Pacific crossings to a then still mysterious Asia, where he ran with the likes of Her British Majesty's agent-in-place

L. Ron Hubbard, left, at Congressional Airport, Washington, DC, 1931, with members of George Washington University flying club.

for North China, and the last in the line of Royal Magicians from the court of Kublai Khan. For the record, L. Ron Hubbard was also among the first Westerners to gain admittance to forbidden Tibetan monasteries below Manchuria, and his photographs of China's Great Wall long graced American geography texts.

Upon his return to the United States and a hasty completion of his interrupted high school education, the young Ron Hubbard entered George Washington University. There, as fans of his aerial adventures may have heard, he earned his wings as a pioneering barnstormer at the dawn of American aviation. He also earned a place in free-flight record books for the longest sustained flight above Chicago. Moreover, as a roving reporter for *Sportsman Pilot* (featuring his first professionally penned articles), he further helped inspire a generation of pilots who would take America to world airpower.

Immediately beyond his sophomore year, Ron embarked on the first of his famed ethnological expeditions, initially to then untrammeled Caribbean shores (descriptions of which would later fill a whole series of West Indies mystery-thrillers). That the Puerto Rican interior would also figure into the future of Ron Hubbard stories was likewise no accident. For in addition to cultural studies of the island, a 1932–33

LRH expedition is rightly remembered as conducting the first complete mineralogical survey of a Puerto Rico under United States jurisdiction.

There was many another adventure along this vein: As a lifetime member of the famed Explorers Club, L. Ron Hubbard charted North Pacific waters with the first shipboard radio direction finder, and so pioneered a long-range navigation system universally employed until the late twentieth century. While not to put too fine an edge on it, he also held a rare Master Mariner's license to pilot any vessel, of any tonnage in any ocean.

Yet lest we stray too far afield, there is an LRH note at this juncture in his saga, and it reads in part:

"I started out writing for the pulps, writing the best I knew, writing for every mag on the stands, slanting as well as I could."

To which one might add: His earliest submissions date from the summer of 1934, and included tales drawn from true-to-life Asian adventures, with characters roughly modeled on British/American intelligence operatives he had known in Shanghai. His early Westerns were similarly peppered with details drawn from personal experience. Although therein lay a first hard lesson from the often cruel world of the pulps. His first Westerns were soundly rejected as lacking the authenticity of a Max Brand yarn

Capt. L. Ron Hubbard in Ketchikan, Alaska, 1940, on his Alaskan Radio Experimental Expedition, the first of three voyages conducted under the Explorers Club flag.

(a particularly frustrating comment given L. Ron Hubbard's Westerns came straight from his Montana homeland, while Max Brand was a mediocre New York poet named Frederick Schiller Faust, who turned out implausible six-shooter tales from the terrace of an Italian villa).

Nevertheless, and needless to say, L. Ron Hubbard persevered and soon earned a reputation as among the most publishable names in pulp fiction, with a ninety percent placement rate of first-draft manuscripts. He was also among the most prolific, averaging between seventy and a hundred thousand words a month. Hence the rumors that L. Ron Hubbard had redesigned a typewriter for faster keyboard action and pounded out manuscripts on a continuous roll of butcher paper to save the precious seconds it took to insert a single sheet of paper into manual typewriters of the day.

That all L. Ron Hubbard stories did not run beneath said byline is yet another aspect of pulp fiction lore. That is, as publishers periodically rejected manuscripts from top-drawer authors if only to avoid paying top dollar, L. Ron Hubbard and company just as frequently replied with submissions under various pseudonyms. In Ron's case, the list

A Man of Many Names

Between 1934 and 1950, L. Ron Hubbard authored more than fifteen million words of fiction in more than two hundred classic publications. To supply his fans and editors with stories across an array of genres and pulp titles, he adopted fifteen pseudonyms in addition to his already renowned L. Ron Hubbard byline.

Winchester Remington Colt
Lt. Jonathan Daly
Capt. Charles Gordon
Capt. L. Ron Hubbard
Bernard Hubbel
Michael Keith
Rene Lafayette
Legionnaire 148
Legionnaire 14830
Ken Martin
Scott Morgan
Lt. Scott Morgan
Kurt von Rachen
Barry Randolph
Capt. Humbert Reynolds

included: Rene Lafayette, Captain Charles Gordon, Lt. Scott Morgan and the notorious Kurt von Rachen—supposedly on the lam for a murder rap, while hammering out two-fisted prose in Argentina. The point: While L. Ron Hubbard as Ken Martin spun stories of Southeast Asian intrigue, LRH as Barry Randolph authored tales of

L. Ron Hubbard, circa 1930, at the outset of a literary career that would finally span half a century.

romance on the Western range—which, stretching between a dozen genres is how he came to stand among the two hundred elite authors providing close to a million tales through the glory days of American Pulp Fiction.

In evidence of exactly that, by 1936 L. Ron Hubbard was literally leading pulp fiction's elite as president of New York's American Fiction Guild. Members included a veritable pulp hall of fame: Lester "Doc Savage" Dent, Walter "The Shadow" Gibson, and the legendary Dashiell Hammett—to cite but a few.

Also in evidence of just where L. Ron Hubbard stood within his first two years on the American pulp circuit: By the spring of 1937, he was ensconced in Hollywood, adopting a Caribbean thriller for Columbia Pictures, remembered today as *The Secret of Treasure Island.* Comprising fifteen thirty-minute episodes, the L. Ron Hubbard screenplay led to the most profitable matinée serial in Hollywood history. In accord with Hollywood culture, he was thereafter continually called

The 1937 Secret of Treasure Island, *a fifteen-episode serial adapted for the screen by L. Ron Hubbard from his novel,* Murder at Pirate Castle.

upon to rewrite/doctor scripts—most famously for long-time friend and fellow adventurer Clark Gable.

In the interim—and herein lies another distinctive chapter of the L. Ron Hubbard story—he continually worked to open Pulp Kingdom gates to up-and-coming authors. Or, for that matter, anyone who wished to write. It was a fairly unconventional stance, as markets were already thin and competition razor sharp. But the fact remains, it was an L. Ron Hubbard hallmark that he vehemently lobbied on behalf of young authors—regularly supplying instructional articles to trade journals, guest-lecturing to short story classes at George Washington University and Harvard, and even founding his own creative writing competition. It was established in 1940, dubbed the Golden Pen, and guaranteed winners both New York representation and publication in *Argosy*.

But it was John W. Campbell Jr.'s *Astounding Science Fiction* that finally proved the most memorable LRH vehicle. While every fan of L. Ron Hubbard's galactic epics undoubtedly knows the story, it nonetheless bears repeating: By late 1938, the pulp publishing magnate of Street & Smith was determined to revamp *Astounding Science Fiction* for broader readership. In particular, senior editorial director F. Orlin Tremaine called for stories with a stronger *human element*. When acting editor John W. Campbell balked, preferring his spaceship-driven tales,

Tremaine enlisted Hubbard. Hubbard, in turn, replied with the genre's first truly *character-driven* works, wherein heroes are pitted not against bug-eyed monsters but the mystery and majesty of deep space itself—and thus was launched the Golden Age of Science Fiction.

The names alone are enough to quicken the pulse of any science fiction aficionado, including LRH friend and protégé, Robert Heinlein, Isaac Asimov, A. E. van Vogt and Ray Bradbury. Moreover, when coupled with LRH stories of fantasy, we further come to what's rightly been described as the foundation of every modern tale of horror: L. Ron Hubbard's immortal *Fear*. It was rightly proclaimed by Stephen King as one of the very few works to genuinely warrant that overworked term "classic"—as in: *"This is a classic tale of creeping, surreal menace and horror. . . . This is one of the really, really good ones."*

L. Ron Hubbard, 1948, among fellow science fiction luminaries at the World Science Fiction Convention in Toronto.

To accommodate the greater body of L. Ron Hubbard fantasies, Street & Smith inaugurated *Unknown*—a classic pulp if there ever was one, and wherein readers were soon thrilling to the likes of *Typewriter in the Sky* and *Slaves of Sleep* of which Frederik Pohl would declare: *"There are bits and pieces from Ron's work that became part of the language in ways that very few other writers managed."*

And, indeed, at J. W. Campbell Jr.'s insistence, Ron was regularly drawing on themes from the Arabian Nights and so introducing readers to a world of genies, jinn, Aladdin and Sinbad—all of which, of course, continue to float through cultural mythology to this day.

At least as influential in terms of post-apocalypse stories was L. Ron Hubbard's 1940 *Final Blackout*. Generally acclaimed as the finest anti-war novel of the decade and among the ten best works of the genre ever authored—here, too, was a tale that would live on in ways few other writers

imagined. Hence, the later Robert Heinlein verdict: "Final Blackout *is as perfect a piece of science fiction as has ever been written.*"

Like many another who both lived and wrote American pulp adventure, the war proved a tragic end to Ron's sojourn in the pulps. He served with distinction in four theaters and was highly decorated

Portland, Oregon, 1943; L. Ron Hubbard captain of the US Navy subchaser PC 815.

for commanding corvettes in the North Pacific. He was also grievously wounded in combat, lost many a close friend and colleague and thus resolved to say farewell to pulp fiction and devote himself to what it had supported these many years—namely, his serious research.

But in no way was the LRH literary saga at an end, for as he wrote some thirty years later, in 1980:

"Recently there came a period when I had little to do. This was novel in a life so crammed with busy years, and I decided to amuse myself by writing a novel that was pure science fiction."

That work was *Battlefield Earth: A Saga of the Year 3000*. It was an immediate *New York Times* bestseller and, in fact, the first international science fiction blockbuster in decades. It was not, however, L. Ron Hubbard's magnum opus, as that distinction is generally reserved for his next and final work: The 1.2 million word *Mission Earth*.

> **Final Blackout**
> *is as perfect a piece of science fiction as has ever been written.*
>
> —Robert Heinlein

How he managed those 1.2 million words in just over twelve months is yet another piece of the L. Ron Hubbard legend. But the fact remains, he did indeed author a ten-volume *dekalogy* that lives in publishing history for the fact that each and every volume of the series was also a *New York Times* bestseller.

Moreover, as subsequent generations discovered L. Ron Hubbard through republished works and novelizations of his screenplays, the mere fact of his name on a cover signaled an international bestseller. . . . Until, to date, sales of his works exceed hundreds of millions, and he otherwise remains among the most enduring and widely read authors in literary history. Although as a final word on the tales of L. Ron Hubbard, perhaps it's enough to simply reiterate what editors told readers in the glory days of American Pulp Fiction:

He writes the way he does, brothers, because he's been there, seen it and done it!

THE STORIES FROM THE GOLDEN AGE

Your ticket to adventure starts here with the Stories from the Golden Age collection by master storyteller L. Ron Hubbard. These gripping tales are set in a kaleidoscope of exotic locales and brim with fascinating characters, including some of the most vile villains, dangerous dames and brazen heroes you'll ever get to meet.

The entire collection of over one hundred and fifty stories is being released in a series of eighty books and audiobooks. For an up-to-date listing of available titles, go to www.goldenagestories.com.

AIR ADVENTURE

FAR-FLUNG ADVENTURE

SEA ADVENTURE

TALES FROM THE ORIENT

The Devil—With Wings	*Pearl Pirate*
The Falcon Killer	*The Red Dragon*
Five Mex for a Million	*Spy Killer*
Golden Hell	*Tah*
The Green God	*The Trail of the Red Diamonds*
Hurricane's Roar	*Wind-Gone-Mad*
Inky Odds	*Yellow Loot*
Orders Is Orders	

MYSTERY

The Blow Torch Murder	*The Grease Spot*
Brass Keys to Murder	*Killer Ape*
Calling Squad Cars!	*Killer's Law*
The Carnival of Death	*The Mad Dog Murder*
The Chee-Chalker	*Mouthpiece*
Dead Men Kill	*Murder Afloat*
The Death Flyer	*The Slickers*
Flame City	*They Killed Him Dead*

135

FANTASY

Borrowed Glory
The Crossroads
Danger in the Dark
The Devil's Rescue
He Didn't Like Cats

If I Were You
The Last Drop
The Room
The Tramp

SCIENCE FICTION

The Automagic Horse
Battle of Wizards
Battling Bolto
The Beast
Beyond All Weapons
A Can of Vacuum
The Conroy Diary
The Dangerous Dimension
Final Enemy
The Great Secret
Greed
The Invaders

A Matter of Matter
The Obsolete Weapon
One Was Stubborn
The Planet Makers
The Professor Was a Thief
The Slaver
Space Can
Strain
Tough Old Man
240,000 Miles Straight Up
When Shadows Fall

WESTERN

The Baron of Coyote River
Blood on His Spurs
Boss of the Lazy B
Branded Outlaw
Cattle King for a Day
Come and Get It
Death Waits at Sundown
Devil's Manhunt
The Ghost Town Gun-Ghost
Gun Boss of Tumbleweed
Gunman!
Gunman's Tally
The Gunner from Gehenna
Hoss Tamer
Johnny, the Town Tamer
King of the Gunmen
The Magic Quirt

Man for Breakfast
The No-Gun Gunhawk
The No-Gun Man
The Ranch That No One Would Buy
Reign of the Gila Monster
Ride 'Em, Cowboy
Ruin at Rio Piedras
Shadows from Boot Hill
Silent Pards
Six-Gun Caballero
Stacked Bullets
Stranger in Town
Tinhorn's Daughter
The Toughest Ranger
Under the Diehard Brand
Vengeance Is Mine!
When Gilhooly Was in Flower

137

Unleash All the Thrills of Flight!

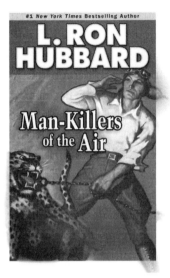

Take a touch of Charles Lindbergh, mix in a dash of Evel Knievel, throw in one man-killing cat—and you've got a recipe for adventure featuring the high-flying, hard-living Smoke Burnham. Now, he's in a life-and-death race in pursuit of big money... and big trouble. Because one thing you can count on—in the air, in a fight or in his girlfriend's arms—where there's Smoke, there's fire.

Set a course for the Andes and the Amazon as the audio version of *Man-Killers of the Air* takes you on a death-defying flight from heaven to hell and back again.

Get

Man-Killers of the Air

PAPERBACK: $9.95 OR AUDIOBOOK: $12.95

Free Shipping & Handling for Book Club Members

CALL TOLL-FREE: 1-877-8GALAXY (1-877-842-5299)

OR GO ONLINE TO **www.goldenagestories.com**

Galaxy Press, 7051 Hollywood Blvd., Suite 200, Hollywood, CA 90028

JOIN THE PULP REVIVAL
America in the 1930s and 40s

Pulp fiction was in its heyday and 30 million readers were regularly riveted by the larger-than-life tales of master storyteller L. Ron Hubbard. For this was pulp fiction's golden age, when the writing was raw and every page packed a walloping punch.

That magic can now be yours. An evocative world of nefarious villains, exotic intrigues, courageous heroes and heroines—a world that today's cinema has barely tapped for tales of adventure and swashbucklers.

Enroll today in the Stories from the Golden Age Club and begin receiving your monthly feature edition selected from more than 150 stories in the collection.

You may choose to enjoy them as either a paperback or audiobook for the special membership price of $9.95 each month along with FREE shipping and handling.

CALL TOLL-FREE: 1-877-8GALAXY
(1-877-842-5299) OR GO ONLINE TO
www.goldenagestories.com
AND BECOME PART OF THE PULP REVIVAL!

Prices are set in US dollars only. For non-US residents, please call
1-323-466-7815 for pricing information. Free shipping available for US residents only.

Galaxy Press, 7051 Hollywood Blvd., Suite 200, Hollywood, CA 90028